CHARLEY AND THE LAST CAVALIERS

J F HARDEN JR.

ISBN: 978-1-4269-4674-5 (sc)
ISBN: 978-1-4269-4678-3 (e)

Trafford rev. 04/18/2011

 www.trafford.com

North America & international
toll-free: 1 888 232 4444 (USA & Canada)
phone: 250 383 6864 ♦ fax: 812 355 4082

PREFACE

They were two young men, both still in their teens and both from the same community. Schooled together, they had remained close friends after finishing the eighth grade. These last few years they'd worked, each helping on their own families farms. Now with their younger brothers and sisters old enough to take over, they could leave. Their parents and other relatives would have all the help they needed.

For years they had joined together as adventurous youths, now they talked of more exciting things to do, and places to see. Though they were warned about how tough the times were, and that there was little work, except for seasonal farm labor, they were not deterred. They had heard of the new courthouse being built in St. Louis. Though it was some distance away, and was a place they had never been, they felt sure a city with that large a building project would surely need many workers.

Their families, though reluctant to see them leave, did help them gather the things they would need. They knew these were determined young men anxious to look for that something they felt in their hearts was out there, waiting just for them.

They would ride west to St. Louis and end up farther west then either would have ever anticipated.

Chapter I

They stopped at the courthouse that was being built to ask about work. Obvious by their dress that they were fresh off the farm, they were told there were no jobs for unskilled labor. The man there did tell them they could probably find work, cutting firewood, along the river. "Just follow the river; you're sure to find some wood hawk that needs help."

The trees close to the town were pretty well depleted. They would have to travel down river some distance before there would be enough trees left to support a wood- cutting operation. Too late in the day to travel much farther, they found a decent spot to spend the night, stopped, and made their camp.

A small fire was made from sticks they gathered. Biscuits and bacon bought in St. Louis would be their supper; they talked about what they knew they were in for. Farm boys with no real skills, it was going to be a rough road ahead for sure. But they assured each other they'd do it. They were used to hard work, and chopping wood wouldn't be something new. Watching the river as their fire burned down, they enjoyed a peaceful night. Morning, and it was more biscuits and bacon, and Tom telling Fran that this diet could get old quick.

Riding south and parallel to the river, they had only ridden for a mile or so before coming onto trees. Here they found a new camp being set up. A grizzled older man by what was surely a cook tent, and dining room told them that, yes, it was a woodcutter camp.

Invited for coffee, they were told there might be jobs here, but he was just the cook and straw boss. "I'm Charlie Teasdale; the boss is Ed Burke." He's down on the beach with the cordwood waiting for the boat. "You finish your coffee, and we'll go down and check," he told them.

1

"My partner is Tom Thorne, and I'm Fran Leon," Fran told Charley, we'd sure appreciate it." "Could use some work could you?" Charley asked. "We could," Fran answered.

Down near the edge of the river they found Ed Burke sitting on the wagon tongue, his horse grazing nearby. Introduced to him by Charley, he said, "yes, he could use more hands. "Tell them what's expected of them, Charley, and what their cut will be, then get them to work." He shook their hands, a man with large soft hands and sweaty palms. A big man yet fairly portly, that and his weak handshake might well obscure the fact that here was a big powerful man that could be difficult to reckon with.

Someone, who was surely enjoying his life, but did over indulging in the very things that would eventually put him down. But for right now Fran knew he would have to respect the man for what he was, but something told him to be wary.

Charley told them they would get a share of what each cord of wood sold for, the same as the others. "Ed owns the camp, and buys the supplies." "I take care of the cooking; plus, the wagon and team we use to haul with, belongs to me."

Out in the woodlot to where the others were working, and Charlie introduced them to Bob Pine, Andy Bender, and Hank Pilcher. The axes, and saws were there, and they put their horses out on pickets and went to work. It would take them just a short time to fall into the rhythm of how things worked. They took turns on the saws, axes, loading the wagon, and then stacking the wood in cords on the beach. It was hard work but the kind of labor most farm boys were used to.

Charley prepared good meals, and in the evenings at their table would tell them stories about the years past, when he trapped. It was a good life he told them, but it was really only for younger men. Those young fellows who could suffer through the cold winters in the mountains, plus work in the ice-cold water with his traps.

The young men were always anxious to hear his tales about the Indians. And of course; he'd tell them about some close calls he'd had. But he made it clear that the Indians, for the most part, weren't all that bad. But there was a bad apple now and then, but no more then with any other folks. "Course it's a might different when you rile one of them. "You know killing someone who's not from their tribe could get him a feather for his bonnet, not a noose for his neck."

Charley liked his Sundays off, telling them the Lord wanted them to respect that day. Most Sundays they did take the time to do some hunting, fishing, or working with their own horses. But some times Ed wouldn't leave for the weekend. He'd stay and drink at his personal tent, and insist they get more wood down onto the beach.

Depleting the trees in one area would require them to move, always to where there were more trees, and a suitable beach. Again they would stack the cordage they cut, and the boats would come in to pick up this fuel they needed. Moving meant there would be no wood to cut for a day or two, consequently nothing earned during those days. Sometimes they'd even have to grade a wagon road to the beach, requiring more labor without pay. This they understood was necessary, something that had to be done. The wood couldn't sell, if it wasn't where the boats could get it.

There were something's that bothered them; one was there always seemed to be a discrepancy between the numbers of cords they cut and the number they were paid for. Bob Pine always kept a notched stick tally for the cords they'd cut. But Ed paid them according to what he said was his count.

Getting together they decided they'd ask Ed about the difference in the count. After supper, Bob told Ed that there always seemed to be a difference between their tally, and the count they were being paid for.

Ed's face already florid from whatever he'd been drinking turned livid. Standing up he reached across the table, but Bob was to fast. "I'll break your neck you damn little runt," Ed shouted, "accusing me of something like that."

"He didn't accuse you", Fran said, "he was just asking".

"And you, I knew you were trouble when you came begging for a job," Ed said, pointing his finger at Fran. "I didn't beg you for nothing", Fran answered. "Hold everything right there," Charley said. "Let's just back off this thing for now, tomorrow I'll start keeping count." "Arguing is just going to conjure up a lot of hard feelings."

Ed stood up kicking his chair out of the way, his face now purple with rage, and stalked out of the cook tent.

"He might fire all of us," Andy said. "I don't think so," Charley answered, "he knows we could start selling wood tomorrow anyplace along the river."

"How about his contacts?" Andy asked.

"Those boats might contract for a low price, but that's it," Charley told them. "When they need wood for them boilers, they ain't particular whose wood they burn."

Ed's becoming so belligerent because of Bob's question didn't set too well with any of the young men, but they all felt with Charley taking the reins, things should work out all right.

They were putting money away, more from not being able to get to town then from being paid a lot. But now and then they did buy some things from of the roustabouts or crewmen off the steamboats. Most of them wanting to buy the newer percussion rifles and pistols. Their old flintlocks so unreliable in wet weather, and pistols, now with five or six shots, though maybe not as accurate as some singles, were much preferred.

Whiskey was always available from the boats, but Charley kept them in line, and they could also see what liquor was doing to Ed. He was getting worse now, staying in his tent for days some times or going into St. Louis and not coming back for a week.

Charley always made sure Ed paid their shares when he came back to camp. Once, Charley said that Ed couldn't be drinking all his money up, he's got to be gambling or chasing or maybe both.

They worked every day but Sundays. But then Ed taking on more work was making it difficult, yet Charley wanted them to have their Sundays off.

Sundays someone usually wanted to go hunting or fishing, then maybe if they were lucky, there would be a brief respite from their regular fare of biscuits, gravy, hominy grits, beans or cornmeal fixed one way or another.

Some Sundays they even tried some target shooting. Sharpening their eye, they told Charley. They did do some betting but soon quit that, when Fran kept winning all the money. For some reason, he had that little extra that made him hard to beat.

More cords of wood, and those steamboats seemed to keep the beach cleared no matter how much they cut and stacked. Money was coming in, but Charley told them they would never be rich. They were working hard, but they were enjoying themselves too, because right then they were having no real problems.

Then Ed came back to camp, and spent two days alone in his own tent before going down to take care of the beach. Four days he collected the money as the boats hauled away the cords of wood. On the fifth morning he was starting to town when Charley asked him, "where he was heading?"

"If I thought it was any of your business, old man," Ed told him, "I'd tell you."

"Are you going to pay the boys their cut?" Charley asked.

"I'll settle later," Ed, answered.

"You said you'd pay when the money came in, Ed," Charley said. "That's what you agreed to." "Now you do what you promised."

"I'm going to give you something I should have given you a long time ago, Charley," Ed said, as he started forward.

Fran stepped in front of Charley. Stopping, Ed said, "You want what I'm going to give him, kid?"

"Is that a challenge?" Fran asked.

"You damn right," Ed answered.

"Then it's my choice of weapons," Fran answered. "You've got a pistol on your hip, Ed. Use it, and we'll settle this now."

Ed grew pale; he'd seen what Fran could do with that pistol, and knew he'd be no match for him. He turned, got up on his buggy, and whipped his horse into a gallop, heading into town.

"Thanks," Charley said, "that could have gotten serious."

"I was pretty sure he wouldn't try anything," Fran said. "He's the kind that needs all the advantages." "But, I guess I've crossed that line, Charley." "I'll pack my gear and move on."

"Not yet," Charley answered. "Let's just see what happens."

The rest of the crew was there now, and they mulled it over, and came to the same conclusion as Charley.

Everyone went back to work; there was a boat on the beach. They'd picked up what was there, and said they'd come back later for more.

They worked for a week with no sign of Ed. "He had a pretty good pocket full of jingle," Charley told them at breakfast, "probably having himself a real good time."

They were barely into their work when they heard the steam whistle on the boat coming in—one loud earsplitting blast after another. They headed to the beach wondering what all the noise was about.

On the beach, the roustabouts were running, taking the wood aboard. "Got to get going," one of them said. "We want to go hear more about the gold strike in California." They helped the crew load the wood. Charley collected the money, and they walked up to the cook tent to talk.

"If it's big," Charley said, "there's going to be thousands of people heading out there." "Everyone wants to be a millionaire."

"Me, for one," Hank said." Let's go." They talked about it for a while, and the young men all agreed it would be up to Charley. He was the one who'd been out that way. If he would lead them, they'd pack up and go.

"I can get us into the Rocky Mountains," Charley told them, "but beyond there, I just don't know."

5

"We can find the trail; there's been others who've gone there." "There's sure to be marks on the trail we can follow," Hank said, all excited. They all knew he, for one, was surely ready to go.

It was Charley who knew the rigors of that trail, and the pitfalls. That's why he was where he was now. But, buoyed by these young men, he knew they were the strength that could get them through.

He listened to them for a while and then said, "All right, we go. But there's things that have to be done; we need things for the trail that we don't have now."

They worked on the list of things they would need to make such an arduous journey. With their list, Charley said he'd go in and purchase the items except the horses; those they'd trade for after they reached Independence. "I'm going to try to find Ed and give him his share of what we've collected," Charley said. "Why?" Hank asked. "He didn't."

"I'll hold out for what he ran off with, but I'm not going to be like him." "I just ain't like that."

"Better take Fran with you, then," Hank suggested.

"I don't think he'll try anything when he's in town," Charley told them.

"You go ahead, cut and sell as much as you can until I get back." "Then we'll leave," he said, as he headed for town. They worked feverishly, trying to cut and sell all the wood they could. It was extra money they'd surely need along the way or when they reached California, plus, it would sustain them while hunting for that precious metal.

Charley was gone all the rest of that day, and they had to fend for themselves. They were worried when Charley didn't show up that night. Morning, and Charley still wasn't back. They were worried, but they would wait until noon before going to check.

Hank and Fran were ready to saddle their horses when Charley came rolling in. Hardly anything on the wagon, and they thought that maybe something had happened, and he was canceling out. When they asked if everything was still all right, he said, "that everything was fine, but he did change things a bit."

"Tomorrow we ride into town and deliver the wagon to its new owner," Charley said. "Then we ride for Independence." "Without the wagon, our trail time will be cut in half." "I shipped everything ahead; the only thing we're short of is horses, and when we pick up that gear we'll have to have pack animals."

Morning they were heading into town, and now Fran, like the others who had purchased percussion rifles, found that carrying two rifles while on horseback was not only difficult but almost impossible. Charley, seeing their frustration, told them to trade that extra rifle for a horse. "I know it can be like shucking off a faithful old friend, but you'll be doing it sooner or later, believe me."

It took some time, but the people preparing for the trail needed arms. Not to many would ride; most would walk along with their wagons. It did take a while, but they soon had enough packhorses to move on to Independence. There they could finish rounding out their string.

They didn't find Ed; he found them, half drunk, ugly, and mad as hell that they were all leaving. He knew he was all finished as a wood hawk, unless he wanted to do it all himself. Trying to muster a crew of woodcutters now would be difficult, if not impossible. Most able-bodied men were thinking about the gold they could be gleaning from some stream in the mountains of California. That chance against the pittance they'd be paid for their labor, sweating with axe and saw, would be a damned hard sell for Ed.

Charley listened to Ed ranting and cussing until he drew a crowd. Then told him where he left his share from the last wood sold. Mounting, he led his young entourage out of town, and onto the road to Independence.

This was his time to see, where each of his young wards were going to fit in. What they were capable of and where their weaknesses were. He pushed them and the horses hard for the next four days. Determined to find any weak links, be it man or horse, before they hit that long trail.

The next days, Charley cooked only once a day; and they ate hot corndodgers and coffee. At noon, and at supper, they ate the now cold corndodgers that he'd fried in the morning. But their coffee was hot at every meal. They hoped and prayed this wasn't going to be their fare for the whole two thousand miles to California.

Reaching Independence, they set up camp, and Charley thanked them for bowing their necks and hanging in there. "I had to know," he told them, "that each of you, and your horses could cut it." "From here to Fort Bridger, barring the weather or some Injun looking to steal a horse, we'll do fine." "After that it's going to be as new to me as it is to you, but we will do it; I've got faith in that."

They picked up the things Charley had sent ahead, then worked two days getting their packhorses- saddles, and packs all ready. Charley checked everything, and had them correct every little flaw he found.

Chapter II

He rousted them out early with his fire blazing, and the coffee boiling. Their horses – saddled; they were all ready in the first light before the sun broke over the horizon. In the saddle, Charley led out, and they fell in behind him, not any particular order.

But they were soon riding side by side where they could—palavering some, as Charley called it. The grass now up, showing nice and green. This was the Oregon Trail they were following, two wagon wheel tracks easily followed.

Wagons ahead of them somewhere. Maybe starting for Oregon, but surely some of them would change their destination when they heard that gold had been discovered in California.

Only on the trail a few days, they passed the first of the wagon trains they'd overtake. It was early in the day, and Charley just waved as they rode by. "They can't know anymore about things than we do," he said.

At first it was just a misty rain but enough that they broke out the oiled canvas capes Charley had purchased for each of them. Every packsaddle was also covered with the same, protecting their loads from whatever— rain right now, but surely dust later on. They found the wagon trail soft from the rain, and Charley told them that could be a real problem for the wagons. Those heavily loaded wagons are just not going to roll easily on a soft trail.

They moved off the trail, the horses moving easier over the undisturbed ground. At their night camps they took care to make sure the gear was up off the wet ground. Little firewood, and the cow or buffalos chips wet, they had only brush broken into pieces to cook or boil coffee water.

The next wagon train they passed was making little headway along that soggy trail, their wheels sinking in the wet ground. They rode slightly away from the trail, not deviating from their line of travel, and simply waved at these people, as they had the others, and rode on.

They stayed in the saddle for as many hours as they could, and their camps were miserable. Their fires greedily consuming the sparse sticks and twigs they gathered, burned rapidly and producing little heat. It was a must though they take the time to let their horses graze, imperative that the animals maintain their strength.

Though it didn't rain all the time, it never stopped long enough for the land to dry. Charley broke away from the wagon trail, angling a little to the north, following a trail, game, Indian and or buffalo.

He told them, "We need to take a little time to dry out. Cook us a decent meal, maybe even do a little hunting." The trail was climbing, and ahead they could see a ridge that looked like it had some trees on it.

Game had been scarce, but now on this higher ground they saw sign. Charley stopped under some trees; here they could put up a tarp for cover, and there was ample wood for a decent fire.

"Get your rifle," he told Fran. "The others can set up camp. Let's go see about some fresh meat." Riding to a wash, he told Fran to cross over, then to watch along the sides for deer. "They'll try to sneak away through the brush or stand real still trying to hide," Charley said. "No does; they'll have a fawn with them this time of year." "Look for horns, the bucks should be in velvet now, so you watch for them sneaking out." Fran brought the little buck down with one well-placed shot. They put it over the saddle, the stirrup up so the blood would fall on the ground and not on any part of the saddle leather.

Back in camp, they had it cleaned and skinned in just minutes, everyone ready for a taste of fresh meat. First it was a little bacon in their fry pan for grease, then the slices of fresh liver. They would eat heartily this evening. This meal and what they would consume for breakfast. Then there would be some left for lunch, supper that evening, and some that Charley cooked until it was dry.

Better find a bigger one next time, they told Fran, that one wasn't much more than a big rabbit.

With the meat that had been cooked, and the corndodgers Charley had fried, they'd get by for a couple of days.

Up early, there wasn't a lot of interest in breakfast, everyone having eaten more than they should have at supper the night before.

Angling down and to the southwest, they would pick up the wagon trail quite a distance ahead of where they'd left it.

The rain had stopped, but the sky still looked ominous, with dark clouds overhead—boiling smoky black. "She's going to come down again," Charley told them, and it did.

Coming on another wagon train, this one bogged down, and by the odor they knew it had been there for close to a week. There were crosses close by, and as they came closer they saw the black cloths draped at the rear of some of the wagons. A rider came out to talk, but maintained his distance.

"Better stay clear," he said. "We've got a sickness among us."

"Whatever you have, mister, you're wallowing in; get your people away from the filth, that they're right in the middle of now, "Charley told him.

"Our teams can't move the wagons," the man complained.

"Hook up as many teams as it takes to move one wagon. Move them one at a time, but for your own sake, get them moved."

"We'll try," he said, and rode away.

Charley rode on, shaking his head, and muttering something about the fools that the Lord has put on this earth. *But there's nothing we can do that they can't do on their own*, he thought.

The trail ahead was clear; there were no signs of wagons passing over it for some time. "That must have been the first bunch of wagons to leave Independence this spring," he said.

For the next two days they heard Charley muttering things like, "How could the Lord put people like that down here," or, "Who told the damn fools they had brains enough to cross this country?" They knew the trouble that those people back there were in was bothering him; he was worried, and frustrated. But short of going back and taking over the wagon train, there was nothing he could do about it.

Another day and they came up on a group of Indians on the move, men, woman, and children. Charley talked to an older man, who stopped while the others continued moving south. They're looking for buffalo, Charley told his young charges. "I'd like to trade for pemmican with them, but if they're hunting for meat, they're probably getting low on food themselves."

Leaving the Indians with a warning about the wagon train with the sick and dying people, they rode on. Charley later told the others that he had to tell the Indians about the sick people. They'll stay away; they know what the white man's sickness can do to them. They've seen hundreds of their people die from the pox and such.

The spring rains dropped to a trickle; the sun warmed, and they rode now with their spirits high. Grouse and rabbits now seemed to be everywhere. No shooting those little critters, Charley told them, they'd be raising their young now.

"Maybe a young deer or antelope, something we can eat in three or four meals," he said. "But you know, we might buy a dog or two from the next Indians we run across." Charley got no affirmative votes from the others, and he chuckled to himself.

Their leader, they knew, was familiar with the trail, at times going up or down a stream to cross. Better crossings for men on horseback but places impossible for wagons. Needing places where there were better accesses down to the river, and up the other bank.

Meeting six Indian men, Charley stopped, talked to them, dismounted, and ask Fran and the others to gather a bit of wood or chips for a fire. "I want to talk to these folks for a few minutes," he said. The fire built, they boiled coffee, giving some to the Indians while Charley talked.

Picking up to leave, Charley gave each Indian a bit of tobacco. Fran noticing that the Indians had looked them over pretty closely.

As they rode away, he asked Charley about them. "Scouts out looking for buffalo," he told him. "They sure looked us over two or three times," Fran said. "Just their nature," Charley answered, "they don't miss much." "And I'll bet you, they can tell you exactly how many shots each one of us could fire without reloading.'

"You see, things like that interest them," he said.

"You know, I couldn't tell anything by the facial expressions," Fran said. "Kind a dead panned, ain't they Francis, but you watch their eyes, and their hands." "There you can get a lot about how they feel about the question you asked, or the answer you gave them for theirs."

"They don't smile a lot either," Fran said.

"If you mean like a white man, no, they take life a bit more serious." "I've lived around them some," Charley said, "and with them a time or two, some years back." "They live closer to the earth, you might say, but they bathe more than most white folks I ever knew." "They value things different too, so you have to think about some things they do, but don't judge them because of it." "Usually they want to trade for the things they need, but they do like some things like beads and mirrors." "Those come after knives, pots, and things like that." "Whiskey and rifles come first, and in that order."

At Ft. Laramie they took the time to check the horses and gear thoroughly. Charley talked to people there and decided from the information he gathered that they would bypass Fort Bridger.

"We'll take the Sublette cutoff," he told them at supper. "They told me that by going to Ft. Hall, we could miss the Salt Lake desert. Seems there's plenty of desert anyway; no need to suffer any more then we have to."

"Remember, once through South Pass, and over the Rocky Mountains, we'll all be in the same fix. We'll all find some desert to cross."

"That country is as new to me as it is to you. Should be no problem though. We'll be following wagon tracks for most of it."

Charley was rummaging through the packs, saying he couldn't remember which pack the geegaws were in. "What's a Gee Gaw?" Fran asked, smiling."

"Aw, you know," he answered, "the brass tacks, beads, and such we brought to trade with. We'd better pick up some pemmican and jerky before we leave here too. Got to pick up what we can now; there might not be any farther on."

Even though Charley found an acquaintance from years past, he didn't want to spend too much time here. They did their trading and moved on.

Five days later they would leave their marks on Independence Rock. Always concerned about the horses, Charley let them put their mark on the rock while the horses grazed and rested an extra few hours.

Regimented now, they knew the routine, everyone working, taking care of the things that had to be done, without Charley having to concern himself too much. They knew he was taking most of the responsibilities plus the worry, but he'd have it no other way.

Not too many days from Independence Rock, and they were up into South Pass and the Rocky Mountains. Here with the lodge pole pines they had wood for their fires. It was high country, and cooler, but they liked it better than the prairie.

Charley led most of the time, but occasionally, pulling to the side, he'd wave them ahead. Riding in the rear for a while, he could see better how their horses were holding up.

Another week and they reached Fort Hall. Charley went in to check and see if he could find out anything about the trail they'd now follow west. Leaving the others to set up their camp, and take care of the horses.

Quite an encampment of Indians here, and they knew this would probably be their last chance to do some trading. But Charley had told them to wait until he got back. They didn't understand why, until they asked. "Because," he told them, "you may not know what you're buying and end up with a female dependent." They scoffed at that for a minute, and then realized he was right. They knew nothing about the languages these people spoke, and there were probably people from three or four tribes camped here, and all wanting to trade. Then the sign language the Indians used did have some hand signs that could mean something they wouldn't fully understand. Maybe they could buy something then find out later what it actually was. They laughed now but soon came to realize that they could get into trouble by their own ignorant actions. They had some fun teasing each other about who would want to try some trading while the others stood by and watched. But there were no brave hearts among them ready to take a chance with his luck.

With Charley back, they walked together through the different groups of tepees looking at the things the natives hadn't traded to the fort. "Get yourselves a couple pair of moccasins," Charley told them. "They will come in handy later on."

"Something else," he said as they walked," seems the people at the fort were impressed by the way you fellows rode coming in. Nice orderly group, they said; and for a little bit they thought it was an army patrol riding up."

"Is that good?" Hank asked.

"Yep," Charley answered. "Shows you're working together; army calls it discipline."

It took a while to get moccasins for everyone; then, when they were done, Fran asked Charley if he'd go back and help him trade. He wanted a buckskin jacket he saw. An older woman was by the tepee, but a girl of about fifteen or sixteen came out to do the trading. She smiled at Fran as Charley turned to talk to him, after she had told him what she wanted. "Don't take it right off," Charley told Fran. "They lose respect for a person who doesn't work on coming up with a better deal."

Hank and the others kept teasing Fran about not really wanting the jacket that what he really wanted was the girl. They told Charley to talk to her Pop. Wasn't he the one he was going to have to talk to? She knew they were teasing Fran, and smiled even more when she saw him blushing. She was a pretty young girl, that he was sure. The trade for the jacket was made, and she helped him put it on, making him blush even more.

Walking back toward their camp, Fran did look back, and the others started more teasing. Charley, turning toward them, said, "he'd be hard pressed to find a better young woman for a wife." The teasing ceased, and they realized by the tone of Charley's voice there was something more about this they didn't understand, but they would respect Charles's feelings.

Fran was proud of that jacket, with the fringe of buckskin down the back of the sleeves, and wore it in camp that evening.

Charley gave them two canvas water bags each. "Going to need them for the last forty miles of desert," he said. "And those bags are for the horse's water, you'll have to make do with your canteens."

"We 're heading into some tough country," he told them. "Not only the country will be against us. They also told me there's Indians living in that desert country that will steal anything and everything they can put their hands on."

They were all loaded and ready to leave early, having had their breakfast before the sun was up. Fran looked toward the tepee, and as the light improved, he could see her by the fire outside. With the sun barely peeking over the trees on the eastern ridge, they mounted. Looking back, he saw her looking toward them; he had to wave, and she waved back. Fran suddenly saddened by their leaving.

At their first camp, Charley told them it shouldn't be bad for the next maybe four days. After that, and for the next week or so it would be alkali water and a lot of heat. "Then the last day we face will be pure hell," he said. "At times there may be no water, except what we carry, and remember that at those times your horses drink first."

It grew hotter as they dropped down out of the high country. Reaching a stream, Charley told them, "would be the Mary." This they knew was the hot desert country they'd been promised. The water was warm and bad, but it was all there was, and would be all they had for the next week.

After their evening meal, they put their fire out, paired up and spread out, their horse picketed inside their bedding area. "If you hear or see anything during the night," Charley told them, "shoot, don't wait. If you let them get in close, they could spook our horses or put an arrow in one."

Two nights after reaching the stream, they did take a few shots, but they found nothing in the morning. During the day, though, they did see figures trotting along out in the desert.

Charley's care with the horses was paying off now; though they felt they were suffering themselves, their horses remained strong.

They made their camp early, where the stream just disappeared into the swampy area. Their first chore was to put canvas water bags to soak. Then, making camp with the heat pressing down on them, they wished they were back on horseback. At least moving through the hot air seemed better.

The water was bad, but Charley boiled water for coffee and, lacing it with sugar, insisted they all drink their fill. "You're going to need all the water you can hold," he said. "Tomorrow it's going to get rung out of you."

"How about that lake I can see on down the trail?" Andy asked, "Is that good water?"

Charley looked down the trail for a few seconds, then turning said, "That's about the purest you can find, but it's all just hot air you're seeing, nothing but a mirage, Andy." They were all looking, and it did look like a lake. They had seen other mirages but none quite like this one. Maybe it was because they were all just wishing and hoping.

With all the coffee they had to drink, and the oppressive heat all night, no one got much sleep. Charley rousted them out early and got the water boiling for coffee as they saddled the horses. No one felt very hungry, but they did down a couple of corndodgers and as much coffee as they could hold.

As they mounted, Charley said, "We've got to a good early start, but before this day's over our brains are going to fry and our guts are going to boil.

"All right, Andy," Charley said, "you can lead us to that lake you saw."

"Damn," Hank said, "that old man's sure full of vinegar this morning."

"Don't you fret," Fran said. "He's suffering too, but he's sure not going to let you know how much."

They rode until the sun was directly overhead then dismounted and walked a little while to a patch of scrubby grass. Though the grass was poor, Charley said," the rest right now was the important thing." Before moving out on the trail again, they gave each horse the water from the canvas bags.

No getting in the saddled now, Charley led them off walking, and they followed, all determined they would keep up with that tough old bird. For more an hour they walked before Charley mounted, and led them on.

Another two hours, and the horses picked the pace on their own, and had to be restrained. "It's the smell of water," Charley hollered. "Just keep them from breaking into a run." There was no stopping the horses; reaching the river they went right in, and so did the riders. All wallowed around in the cold water until Charley told them to, "get the horses out of the water before they drink too much. Take them up on the grass and get them unsaddled. We can bring them down later for another drink."

With the horses taken care of, they all went down and into the water again. "Good, clear, sweet water right out of the mountains," Charley said. "Thank the Lord we're out of that hell. We've got her whipped, fellas. No more than a week, and we're there." After ducking down in the water, he drank again, walked up by their packs and saddles, and lay down. With his hat over his face and his hands behind his head, Charley lay relaxing in the sun. His clothes still soaked from the dip in the river.

Washing the alkali dust and sweat from their clothes, was a must now, here with good water. Then they'd let them dry overnight draped on nearby bushes. Their camp set up, they would eat a hot but simple meal of boiled jerky and cornbread. "We should be able to come up with some fresh meat tomorrow," Charley told them as they were eating."

With the horse's thirst slaked, and their bellies full of grass. Charley said, "alright fellas lets take the horses down to the river and give them a bath.

Chapter III

They dallied over breakfast and their coffee; Charley was in no hurry now. "We're over the rough part," he said. "Should be a pleasant trail from here on."

Now they talked about the rigors of the trail they'd just traversed. "You had it easy," Charley broke in. "Think about the people coming with those wagons, most of them, man, woman, and child, will be walking that same trail."

"I don't see how they can do it," Andy said.

"They'll be a good many of them sure won't," he told them. Then standing up, he said, "Let's get moving."

"He doesn't even want to think about those folks, does he?" Andy said as he, Fran and Hank walked toward the horses. "Going to be pure hell for them, coming across that stinking desert," Hank answered.

The trail they followed paralleled the river here, brush and grass but groves of leafy trees along the bottoms. With their late start, they would ride for two days before reaching the big pine trees. From here they could look up at the granite peaks they'd soon have to find their way up and over.

Charley sent Fran and Hank after a small herd of deer, telling them to bag a nice yearling. "We need some meat, but only enough for a few meals." It took them a while to finally get what they were sent after. Coming in the camp, it was all set up and the cook fire was going. They fried the liver, but the rest they roasted by the fire. Some they would eat for supper; the rest they roasted well, so it would keep.

They ate heartily and drank the cool water that came from a small stream nearby. It was good coffee they drank now as they sat by the campfire, and here they'd sleep cooler, much closer to the mountains.

They had venison for breakfast with their coffee. After they'd eaten they followed the wagon tracks that led them up through large granite boulders. Along a natural rock bench, that did seem to be leading them up into a dead end. Here they'd see where the wagons went, only by the rusty marks made by the iron rims up a slope that no animal could traverse, except maybe a goat. "They must have used some rope or chain tackle to take the wagons up that slope," Charley told them. Following a natural game trail, they came to a narrow chute that their pack animal could barely fit through. They climbed the steep trail, breaking out on the shoulder of the ridge above.

Stopping to look where the wagons had been brought up, they marveled at what the people had done. "That means they had to carry all their things up through that chute, doesn't it," Fran said. "They must have," Charley answered. "Kind of makes our little trek look easy doesn't it?"

They traveled through something like the Rocky Mountains but more so—large escarpments of granite, and places where they rode over solid rock for a half mile; pine trees, great large ones, and so much bigger than the lodge poles. Grassy meadows, small lakes, and clear, icy, cold streams in every canyon, large or small.

Deer ran away as they approached; ducks flew up from the little lakes, and large, bushy-tailed gray squirrels scolded from the trees as they passed. Little striped squirrels scurried on the ground, which they would learn later were called chipmunks. Then they saw the grouse, with his feather topknot, little fellas called quail.

Their noon stop was in a grassy meadow with a beautiful stream; here they finished the last of the venison with their coffee and cornbread baked in an iron skillet. Andy and Tom both said this would be a good place to spend their summer. "The first wagon train that comes through is sure to run you out when their hungry oxen hit this grass," Charley said. "They'll be half starved before they get here. Now pick up and let's get out of your little piece of paradise and on down toward the valley." They would now and then catch a glimpse of the valley off in the distance.

Charley would not deviate from the main trail, saying those single-track or little-used trails are that way because there's probably a problem with them.

At the first clap of thunder and the lightning flashes, Charley was out of the saddle. He led the group into a sallow draw. There they held the horses as large drops of icy rain pelted them. "It's best to get off the ridges when there's a sudden storm like this," he told them. "If one of those lightning bolts come down, they'll usually hit something that's sticking up higher than what's around them."

Their horses were wild-eyed scared, and if not held in restraint would have bolted and surely run off. It didn't last long, and they were back in the saddle, even through the horses were still a bit skittish.

As they moved lower, the mountain air changed—balmy now, the slight breeze coming up the slope right at them from the valley below. There was more grass here, and fewer pine trees but now a lot of oaks.

Streams ran sparkling in every canyon bottom they looked down into. The trail they followed broke out onto a grassy ridge and then angled down toward the stream below. There they could see men working in the stream, and knew they had to be men looking for gold, just the way they'd soon be.

Reaching the stream, the trail split. One leg followed the stream west toward the valley below; the other led across the stream heading toward the south.

Two men across the stream stood with their riding and packhorses. They watched as Charley and the others approached. Charley, handing the lead rope of his packhorse to Fran, said, "Wait here. I want to talk to those two," and rode across the stream. Dismounting, Charley talked with the men for a few minutes and then waved for Fran to come across. The two men, mounting up, rode south as Fran and the others moved toward them.

On the other side Charley told them, "that the two men were leaving this stream, and heading to a new strike they'd just heard about. "If they're looking for better pickings, I think we might just follow," Charley said. Mounted, and rode south.

Two hours later the sun was down, the two men rode into a grove of trees and dismounted. Charley stopped thirty yards away and said for them to set up camp. He wanted to talk to the two men a bit more. There was good grass, clear water in a small brook, and wood for fire, everything they needed for a good camp. When Charley got back, their coffee pot was already boiling, plus extra water they were sure Charley would need for something, most likely boiling jerky. They hoped that once they reached a somewhat permanent camp they could work toward a more palatable diet.

They talked with Charley about what they felt they needed. He agreed. "I'm tired of what we've had to live on too, but that's what it takes to do what we did," he said. "We've come through in good shape; now after we find a good spot we'll set up a good camp and do a little hunting."

"Tomorrow those fellows told me we'd reach the stream where the new strike was made. We'll figure out then if it's what we want—stay there if it looks promising or move on if not. But whatever we decide, we'll work over our food supply. I'm damned tired of this too." He told them, "but what we've had was a damn sight better than wormy bacon or pickled sowbelly and boiled oatmeal." His young charges were satisfied. They ate their supper, moved the horses to fresh grass, and were retiring to their bedrolls.

As Charley was still frying the corn fritters for their breakfast, they crawled in. After he having told them to go to bed; that he'd finish what needed to get done.

With everything done the evening before, it was simply boil the water for coffee, roll up the bedding, and saddle up. Charley had made enough fritters for the other two men, so they were all on the trail early.

An hour before noon they rode down into a half-mile-wide grassy valley with a stream flowing leisurely down through it. The stream came down out of a steeper rocky slope. Then flowed into this pleasant little grass valley. Here the stream ran clear and cool through the meadowland, two foot deep and three yards wide. A few cottonwoods, and patches of willows grew along the watercourse. Here too a scattering of oaks in the grass flats, and pines on the shoulders of the surrounding hills. It was a much larger and prettier place they thought, than where they'd camped in before up in the high mountains. "Now this is a real piece of paradise," Charley said, stopping to look.

Again Charley left his packhorse with Fran to ride after the two men. Who were now moving up along the stream, headed higher up toward the rocky canyon above. Fran, Hank, Tom, Bob, and Andy rode down to the stream, let the horses drink, then let them graze while they waited for Charley to return.

Fran and Hank walked across the grassy flat while the others soaked up some of the sun. Where the ground began to rise, Hank, seeing a seep, told Fran that could be a spring there. "We should take something and try digging it out," he said. "If there's enough of a spring for camp use, we can camp near it. There we'd be closer to the trees, and a good supply of firewood." They were digging where they figured the source of the seep was when Charley rode up. Wondering what they were up to, he quickly realized when he saw the wet ground that they were digging for water and not gold. He smiled and told them, "I thought for a minute or so that you'd spotted yourself a piece of gold."

They stopped their digging, and watched as the depression they'd dug filled with water. The depression gradually settled out, leaving a pool of cool, clear water. "That's good," Charley said. This is a nice place to set up camp." Then he rode off to tell the others and help gather the horses.

Working together, they soon had the rock gathered for their fire pit, and ample wood for cooking plus for a night fire. While Charley cooked, they built the shelters for their gear, and lean-tos to sleep under, just a little protection from those sudden showers.

Charley did his best with their supper, but it was still boiled jerky and cornbread. Right then it was decided that Fran and Hank would go on a hunt in the morning.

"Tomorrow, Charley said, he'd take Andy with him to where the men were working the stream. They use boxes and things that I've never seen before," he said. "Andy can make a few drawings, then we'll have to go get what we need and make some for our use." That would leave Tom and Bob to watch their camp, and take care of the horses that were left.

Everyone up early anxious to get started, doing what they had come all of this way to do. Fran and Hank, after their coffee and cornbread, rode up toward the forested hills while Charley and Andy followed the stream up to where the men worked the stream. Every one of them up there, working and hoping to find gold enough to make them rich.

Back just a little before noon, Fran and Hank had a small buck plus a nice bunch of onions. They had the buck hung, skinned, and were frying liver with those little wild onions when Charley and Andy rode in. "That sure smells good," Charley said, "but there's sure no time to make biscuits before it's done."

"We can always eat them later," Hank said, "or have them at supper." With not enough liver and onions to satisfy all of them, they fried some steaks, and by then Charley did have biscuits ready.

After eating, they looked at the drawings Andy made and wondered where they could get the lumber they'd need. "We need a lot of things," Charley said, "not only lumber and nails. We've got to find some other things to eat. What we've been living on could make you sick after a time."

"You two," he said to Hank and Fran, "remember where you found those onions. We can use them from time to time, and they can sure help us some."

They had all looked over the drawing Andy made of a cradle, sluice, and Long Tom. With five or six of them working, they could use the Long Tom and process a lot more material, hoping they'd get more gold. The Long Tom was nothing more than a longer sluice, so it could be shortened into a sluice if the need arose.

Charley and Andy worked on the list of things they'd need—not just the lumber and nails, but tools plus food items. Each of them had to come up with as much cash as he could; they needed a lot, and it would be costly, they knew.

The trail they would have to take was the same trail they left when they came down off the mountains. So it was backtrack a ways, then follow that trail down into the broad valley below. There to the large river called the Sacramento and the town with the same name. That round trip might take them a week.

"While we're gone, the first thing the rest of you do is stake out our claims, here on the stream. Then put up a cache where we can store the food so the varmints can't get into it. All right?" Charley said. They all four nodding, sure they had time to get those things done.

Charley and Andy left first thing in the morning, as everyone else headed up to the trees, gathering limbs large and small to haul down into camp, Hank felled four small trees to use for the legs of the cache. They cut and pealed stakes, then hauled them to the north side of the river.

Digging the stakes in only about a foot, they then gathered rocks to stack around them, creating small monuments. By early afternoon the stakes were all in. Afterward they'd bathed in the cold stream, they lay on the grass in the sun to dry.

The next morning, after breakfast, Fran marked where the corner posts should go for the cache, and started digging. Each posthole had to be at least, eighteen inches deep.

He saw a couple of specks of something that looked like flecks of gold. Picking one up, he bent it easily with his fingernails and figured it must be fool's gold.

The cache house itself they built on the ground, splitting small logs for the floor, then cutting notches, and fitting the walls onto the floor. It took them three days to put that cache all together. Everything was done but shingling the roof; and fitting the door. With no nails or pegs in it, they could take it apart, and then reassemble it on top of the four poles after.

Lastly, they cut the rails and rungs for two ladders. They figured it would be a lot easier for two men to work lifting the frame logs into place, and the split logs for the floor. After that, they could both work from that floor platform. All ready now, they only had to wait for nails and rope to haul the pieces up, then tie them in place until they could be nailed.

The work done, Fran and Hank decided maybe a little hunting might be fun. Besides, almost any kind of a change in their diet would be welcome. "I don't think we'd better kill a deer," Fran said. "Some of it would surely go to waste. The four of us could never eat all of it before it went bad."

"Then it's squirrel or maybe grouse," Hank said, "but there's not going to be a lot left of old Bushy tail if he gets hit with a rifle ball."

"Then it's bark him or use a pistol," Fran answered. It was decided then. Hank carried his rifle, but Fran took only his pistol.

Walking together, they headed up into the forested hills there above their campsite. The squirrels were easy enough to find by just walking slowly through the trees. There were large groups plus some smaller ones; these they figured were the young from this spring. Not nearly as wary as the larger, older ones, they would be the ones most likely to fall to these hunters, guns.

Hank barked a large gray that lay flat against a limb, and had just picked it up when he saw Fran pick off a young squirrel. Then he saw Fran turn, as another smaller squirrel started off, hesitated, and paid with its life.

As Fran turned toward him, Hank saw there wasn't a smile of pride at what he'd done, just a look of satisfaction. "He knew he was going to do it," Hank thought. What he saw, Hank knew, was definitely not the norm; he knew he had witnessed his friend do something instinctively. There wasn't time for him to think, he simple acted, just a triggered impulse. From the first flick of movement the squirrel made, to the time the shot was fired, just a split second.

Hank remembered watching Fran working with that pistol as they sat by the fire in the evenings. He wondered why Fran worked on the walnut grips of the pistol so much. There were shallow groves now in the grips—one for his middle, his ring finger, and his little finger. Fran, he realized now, had worked those pistol grips to fit his right hand. Now Hank knew that, like someone pointing his index finger, Fran had added accuracy to that pistol and doing so had added the explosive force of that pistol to his prowess.

Hank, slinging his rifle, then followed Fran as he walked and watched for squirrels. Three more fell to Fran's pistol, but one did get away when he jumped from one tree to another. He just seemed to glide into the canopy of the other tree, and disappear. They knew he was there someplace, but that animal seemed to understand he was safe where he was, now hidden from their sight, it never moved.

Walking back, Fran told Hank, "That was fun wasn't it?"

"I liked it," Hank answered, "but you did seem rather serious, Fran."

"Just pitting myself against him," Fran said. "And it's not all one-sided; you saw that one smart old bushy outfox both of us." Hank felt a bit better now, knowing his friend had not become callous while developing the skill he now possessed.

They cleaned and cut up the squirrels, browned the pieces, then put them in a pot for a stew. The only thing they had to add to the stew, were wild onions. After chopping them up, they tossed them in.

They tried their hand at cornbread, and it didn't come out too bad, just a little too brown on the bottom. Finding some pinecones the squirrels hadn't already gotten, they hit them on flat rocks to get the little nuts out. Not bad at all but small, cones that were probably from last fall and were dark brown. They would have probably been better if they had been gathered in the fall, and the nuts extracted then. It was a twofold benefit though, because the empty cones did burn well.

Chapter IV

They had survived, and seeing them riding across the meadow, they sprinted toward Charley and Andy. Splashing through the stream, they soon had the heavily loaded packhorses in tow, relieving the riders for a minute from that burden.

In camp they unloaded the packs, and unsaddled all the horses. They would take care of things while Charley and Andy took the time to relax with a cup of coffee.

The horses out on pickets, Charley helped them find the things they needed to finish the cache. Hank and Fran now quickly got to work on it. They really needed the protection for their food. Charley was nearby at the campfire cooking, and could tie on the pieces while Fran and Hank worked up on the poles, putting it together. Andy, with Tom and Bob, were busy building the sluice. Two days later they had their foodstuff up in the cache and safe. The sluice was about ready to be put to work.

There was a big improvement in their meals, as Charley even baked apple pies, using dried apples. But they needed meat, so Hank and Fran were destined for the woods just as soon as they finished shingling the roof on the cache.

Men came up the stream and worked in the water below their last claim stakes, but they soon left, going upstream into the canyon above. Most usually coming back down within a day or two. Then heading north or south, most likely to find some other stream to try. Fran and Hank were back from hunting, and the others had the sluice in the water, floating on two logs, and anchored to the shore.

As soon as the buck was skinned, it was bagged to keep the flies and those meat-eating yellow hornets from the meat. Then they walked to the river to watch the others work the gravel through the sluice. They were working hard, first moving rocks, and the top layer of rock and heavy gravel downstream. Then bringing up the bottom gravel and put it in the sluice. They picked out the larger rocks and, lastly, washed the rest across the riffles. They didn't find much that morning and were really glad when Charley said, "soup's on." Their ankles and knees ached from being in the cold water so long.

They brought the sluice onto the shore; then, right after lunch, they cleaned every riffle, finding very little gold. Hank and Fran were there now, so they could move more material through the sluice. But when Charley called them to supper, they pulled the sluice again. Took a quick look, and again saw very little color. At supper they told Charley, and he said, "Then it's bound to get better."

"How can you say that?" Andy asked.

Looking at Andy, Charley smiled and said, "Because it can't get much worse."

Andy didn't think it was all that funny, and Charley said, "Everybody out here just ain't gonna get rich, Andy. Some are going to be lucky to break even. But you be patient." They did a little better as they moved upstream, and figured that it might continue. Andy still was not happy; the work was hard, and the cold water made their legs ache for a long time after they'd gotten out of it.

Each move upstream was only a few feet, but each move meant moving tons of rock and gravel. Every afternoon Andy and Charley washed the fine gravel from the riffle, retrieving little specks of gold. "Think it's worth all this work?" Andy asked. "It all adds up," Charley said.

They had worked weeks before Charley started picking larger pieces of coarse gold out of the riffles. He and Andy kept hiding these, not wanting any of the men who came looking to see how well they were finally doing. The few nuggets that started to appear were quickly picked out and squirreled away. Andy was feeling a lot better now, and working like a beaver.

On Sunday, Charley said, "It's time to take a day off and divide what we've collected so far. With a small scale, Charley and Andy weighed out the gold, and poured each share into a leather pouch. All the pouches were in a pile, and Charley said they could each pick a pouch. He and Andy took the two pouches that were left.

Sunday was a day of rest, but they had their own things to take care of, so it wasn't really all rest. In mid afternoon, Bob walked over to

Charley and told him there was a group of Indians up above the camp. Charley walked to where he could see, and the Indians, knowing they'd been seen, started moving faster up toward the trees. One man looked back, and Charley, using some sign language, got him to stop. After more sign language, the man started walking down cautiously. Charley started walking toward the man, telling Bob, and the others to stay there. "We don't want to scare him off," Charley said.

They watched as Charley and the Indian drew close, still talking with their hands. It took a while, but Charley finally got the man to come in close, and got the others to move slowly down toward the campfire.

Charley and the Indian talked while the others stood a little ways off. There was another man, two women, and two children—a little girl and a small boy—all standing stolidly in a tight little group as the hand-talk went on.

Fran had another chance to look for the geegaws when Charley asked, knowing they had a few things left from their previous trading. "I want to give them a few presents," he told Fran. "This could be our chance to start trading with these people; we need some of the things they eat. Could keep us from getting sick."

Finding the things Charley wanted, Fran saw there wasn't a lot left, but it was probably enough to take care of this small group. Charley took care of parceling the things out, and now sat like Santa Claus giving gifts—a knife for each of the men, a mirror and beads for the women, and some small bells for the children. There were some smiles from the children, and pleased looks from the women. The men seemed somewhat aloof, though they did nod their approval of the presents.

They were talking as they left, walking up toward the trees. Their voices were soft like other Indians they'd heard, different languages of different tribes, but all spoke softly. They didn't seem to have any harsh words that needed to be spoken in a loud voice. But when they asked Charley about it, he told them, "Oh, they can be loud, the men with they're war cries, and the women when they carry on at their funeral wailing.

"Something else," Charley said. "You know, I've never seen a man or woman spank or even scold a child. It seems they have a way of just shaming their children into behaving."

"A lot different than the woodshed, and the old man's razor strop," Fran said, with a far-off look on his face. Charley, looking at Fran, figured he might have experienced that.

They were back in the water in the morning, moving gravel through the sluice, and again the recovery was better. "We're not getting real rich," Charley told them at their noonday break, "but we should come out with a good nest egg. Of course, that's if we keep picking the way we have been."

"I'd just like to get enough so I could go home and pay off our homeplace. Then maybe buy the farm across the road," Andy told them, smiling. "You could maybe do that, all right," Charley answered, "but not a whole lot more."

Then another two days of hard work, but they were happy with the results. It was after they had started on their third day that they saw the same Indians coming down into the camp. They thought it might be two small families, and they would have enjoyed being there while Charley was doing the trading. But they continued with their work. They'd get a look at what Charley traded for at their noon break. The group had walked off toward the forested hills before it was time to stop their work. Then they had to clean out the sluice before they would relax, and warm themselves before eating.

At this meal Charley served some things they hadn't seen before. There were greens, for one thing, that looked like maybe spinach or turnip greens, yet different in a way. Like other young people, they had to study this green food for a few seconds. "Eat it; it's good for you," Charley told them. "Seems to me I've heard someone say that before," Andy said, as he did start eating. "It's all right, I guess," he said, "but I think I could do without it."

"That's what a lot of men think," Charley told him, "but when their teeth start falling out and they're too weak to stand, that's when they realize they were wrong."

There was another dish that they ate with their meat, a kind of little tuber that Charley said, he thought were roots from the rushes that grew in the wetland below.

"I've got some other things," he told them, "but you're going to have to wait until supper time."

Besides picking out the larger pieces of gold as they went, they cleaned the riffles twice every day now. Every move upstream meant more gold they collected, fine, coarse, and nuggets. They were each accumulating multiple pouches, and not just ounces but closer to pounds of gold. Well past the middle of their claims, it wouldn't be many more weeks until it would all come to an end. They started talking about what they were going to do when they were through. Most agreed that they should have enough to do what ever they wanted to do.

The talk of going home was strong among them, but Charley noticed that Fran was the holdout, when it came to talking about a trip back. The other four would go for sure, and they talked about the route they'd take going home. Just from what Andy and Charley had heard on the trip for supplies, the southern route down through California would be their preferred route. It was a trail established many years before by the Spanish, and still being used by the Mexicans and some American traders.

It was desert country much of the way, so it was a preferred winter trail. Even in the winter it was still hot with little water, but still better than the in summer. Some mountain country where they might see a little snow, but nothing to compare with the Sierra or the Rocky mountains.

The Indians, Comanche and Apache both, would be settled in their winter camps, and would be less likely to be plaguing the trail at that time of the year. But either of those tribes could be a problem. They were at that time, the two most hostile tribes in the country. But; Andy said, "We can probably join up with some other travelers and make up a strong group."

They were all young men and well armed, so they would be a welcome addition to any group of travelers.

Hank finally thought to ask Fran, when he saw his friend wasn't showing much interest, "You with us, Fran?"

"No," Fran answered, "I'm going to see that city, San Francisco. It must be my city; it has my name." Visibly concerned, Hank asked Fran to take a walk, and the two young men walked off together. Hank and Fran, Charley knew, had been close friends even before this trip, and he wondered now how this would affect them. They were maturing and, like others, would have to learn to accept disappointments and then continue their lives by stepping over or around the pitfalls they'd encounter like anyone else.

But now Charley wondered about Fran. He was not a loner, but then why hadn't he asked for company? *I guess I'll just have to wait and watch how this all works out*, he thought.

He didn't have long to wait; two days later, after they had finished dividing the last gold they cleaned from the sluice, Fran told them he was going to leave for San Francisco in the morning.

"But we're into the richest part," Hank said. "Aren't you going to stick around for this last week or so?"

"I've got enough I think, to do what I want," Fran answered. "If I had any more I might spend it foolishly," He smiled at his friend. "Work the sluice," he said, "and take what you pick up home with you. You've earned it."

No one tried talking him out of what he said he intended doing. All figuring it would be futile; they knew him pretty well by now.

He asked Charley if he could leave his packhorse. "I don't think I'll need him for this trip."

"Then you're going to come back here?" Charley asked.

"Only if you're going to be here, Charley," he said.

"You know I'll be here," Charley answered. "I haven't seen a better place to put down my roots."

Breakfast finished, they walked to the edge of the stream after shaking Fran's hand. He stood, as he said good-bye to Charley, and mounted. Riding across the stream, he turned and waved. They waved back as he rode away on the trail north, his mount at an easy lope.

They went back into the cold water and to work, but there was a link missing, and it just didn't feel the same. Then, at their noon break, they were to learn something. The last claim they were working was actually Fran's, and, ironically, it was the claim that would produce the most gold.

Having just randomly selected each paper to place at the monument didn't make much difference, since they were going to share and share alike. But on their last day of work they decided if it was all right with Charley. They like to divide that last day's take, with Fran receiving a share. "I'll go along with that, "Charley said, and that share would be left for Fran's return.

Charley helped them get their things together, and made sure everything was in good repair. They didn't need to carry a lot of food on the trail they were going to follow. But Charley insisted they carry dry rations that would keep. "Always carry enough to take care of your needs for a few days," he told them.

They would miss this old man who led them, and watched over them for these many months, but it was going to end now. There was concern for him, but they knew here was an old man that could take care of himself. He'd been doing that, plus watching over and leading them. But now they would miss him sorely.

He stood by his fire and waved as they rode away, realizing that his workload had just diminished significantly, yet he'd miss them. This had been a really special time in his life—a time he would have never dreamt could happen, but it had. He smiled; he had enjoyed every minute, an old man's last fling at life, and now he was at as beautiful a place as an old man could want.

Sitting down, he poured him self a cup of coffee and looked around; he would be lonely for a while. But he'd been there before. Then he did have hope; there was one who said that he'd be back. That alone gave him a good feeling. At this time in his life, with no family, Charley realized what it could mean.

He thought back about the past, but she was gone, and he had elected to face whatever came next alone. Too late now, but he knew he wouldn't have done it differently. But now he'd just wait, live whatever came next, and hope for a good end.

There was work to do, and first he would build a corral for the three horses. He began by felling a few trees.

Chapter V

Riding north, he came to the wagon trail they'd followed down out off the High Sierra. The wagon train he saw Fran knew had crossed the same trail they'd ridden. Gaunt, tired-looking men, women, and children they were, but all smiled; they had made it. He sat his horse thinking about what they had suffered through, and wondered if he could have made that trip as they did, walking all that way.

He shook his head and rode on; as he was passing the wagons he waved back at those people, who smiled and waved to him. They had reason to be happy, he knew. Leaving them behind, he rode on, meeting wagons and men coming up. Heading, he figured, to where they would either sell their goods or look for gold.

On the river they were unloading cargo from boats and barges. Buildings were going up, but there were a lot of tents, and clapboard shacks everywhere. The men here weren't smiling, and most just looked, but some did nod if he greeted them with a smile or wave.

He and his horse would need a ride down the river. He rode down onto a beach where men were unloading cargo. Inquiring at a couple of the boats, and he found one that would haul him and his horse for a fee, but he'd have to take care of cleaning up after his animal. That boat would leave in the morning. He needed now to look for some grain to feed his horse on the boat going down the river. Tonight it was grass for the horse, and a place for him to rest the night. Lying on his bedroll, he could hear the raucous noise from the town, and he heard a couple of shots. Might be a shoot-out or a shoot-up, who knows? Either way, there wouldn't be much done about it.

Loading his horse in the morning was a problem. This horse didn't like the boat, but with some help from the men off the boat the horse was manhandled aboard. With the horse tied up short, he'd have him well under control. He stayed close by the animal throughout the entire trip. A couple of handful of grain now and then seemed to pacify the horse, but he knew his mount wasn't happy aboard this boat.

Numerous sailing ships were at anchor, and Fran wondered why so many ships were offshore. He soon had his answer; there was no one on board those ships. They were derelicts, abandoned by their crews and left to the elements. Each one in it self, worth a small fortune; their crews were now off hunting on their own. Some rich ship owner will lose, and if the sailors don't find gold they'll lose too.

His horse was ready to disembark just as the boat bumped the beach. Fran held him back until the plank was lowered then walked him slowly onto land. Once on the firm beach, the horse shook himself hard enough to rattle the gear he carried.

Four men were lounging at the side of the beach, and Fran wondered about these big, tough-looking men, who seemed to be watching everything and everybody. They sure were not miners loafing here, and though they were on the beach, they didn't seem to be working with any of the boats.

The reins in his left hand, he swung easily up into the saddle; his right hand was close to his side and the butt of his pistol. The men watched Fran closely, and he didn't know exactly what they could be looking for except maybe some miners coming here with a fat poke of gold. "Guess I'd better watch my back trail," he thought.

He rode up the grade to the higher ground, and came on the same hustle and bustle he saw at Sacramento. Here the land wasn't flat; it was rolling and hilly, and there were new buildings everywhere and a lot more going up. There were a pretty high percentage of the same saloons and gambling halls. "I guess it's to be expected," he said to himself. If a man can labor and extract gold from the earth, there's going to be men waiting to relieve him of that burden. He laughed to himself because he was here to spend some of his, but he was determined he'd get as much return as he could for what he had. Right now he was looking for a bank, figuring he'd get as square a deal there as anyplace. He thought he'd cash out about half of what he had; feeling that should be enough to take care of him for quite a while.

It was too late in the day when he did find a bank, so he rode south on a road that led out of the main part of the town. He'd find a place to sleep this night, but right now he was hungry. The road was good and well used, but there was no one on it this late afternoon. A building of mud bricks with an open door and guitar music coming from inside, looked to be the only thing out this way. Tying his horse, he took his rifle with him when he walked in.

A bar, yes, a Mexican bar, and the music stopped when the guitar player saw him. The two men at the bar turned and seemed somewhat surprised. Then the man behind the bar finished wiping his hands, and came around the end of the bar. He motioned to the guitar player then walked up and asked, "Senor can I help you?"

"You speak English?" Fran asked.

"Si, senor, some," he answered.

"Do you serve meals?" Fran asked him.

"What would you like, senor?"

"Anything you have made; I'm not all that fussy, just hungry."

The man motioned to a small table and chairs, close to the door where Fran could see his horse.

"Something to drink?" the man asked.

"Coffee, if you have it," Fran said.

"Chocolate, senor. I do have tequila but no whisky. Your people don't stop here very often, senor."

"But you speak English," Fran said.

"There are quite a few in Monterey who know. I learned because I used to work there when we sold hides, and tallow. But let me get you food, senor, and then maybe we can talk," he said as he left. The guitar player played, and the two men turned back to their drinks.

He brought Fran his meal and asked if they could talk when he finished eating. Nodding, Fran answered, "Sure." The food was good, spicy and hot. The man brought him a bottle, "Cerveza, senor," he asked, smiling. "It will go well with your meal, and one will not bother you." He was right, and Fran enjoyed the beer, and the meal.

After removing the dishes he came to Fran's table, and said his name was Paco. "I'm Fran," Fran answered, "short for Francis. "A good Christian name, senor,"

"I guess so," Fran answered. "And I guess you have some questions to ask."

"Si, senor, I have trouble understand your people who are coming here."

"First, I think many of the people who are coming here now are not my people; many are as foreign to me as they are you," Fran answered.

"Then you are very different, senor," Paco said. "At first I thought you were a pistolero. Second, you asked, you did not demand, like most gringos when they talk to us."

"I don't know what you meant, pistolero?" Fran said. "And I think it's the way a person is brought up. If he's taught to respect others, he will."

"A pistolero, my friend," Paco said, "is a man good with a pistol, and looking at yours, a man can see it is special, and you wear it like it is."

"I guess it is," Fran said, smiling, "but I use it mostly to hunt rabbits and squirrels."

"And what's left of the animal to eat?" Paco asked.

"Everything but the head," Fran told him. "Now I need to find a place to spend the night, and grass my horse." "Anyplace out in the field, Senor."

"Go behind here," Paco told him, "but stay out of the brush; we have a poison plant here that can do you much harm. It has a leaf like an oak tree but not so thick and stiff; don't ever touch it, senor. No one will bother you; I can understand why a man like you might like it out of doors."

"And how about breakfast, Paco?"

"Anytime after the sun comes up, senor."

He saw the bushes in the waning light, and found a small grove of trees to sleep under. It was quiet here, yet he could hear the guitar player singing a sad ballad; though he couldn't understand the words, it had to be what he thought it was.

The air was cool and damp when he got up in the morning, but he had slept well in the cool. After saddling his horse, he tossed his bed over the saddle. It was damp but would dry quickly once the sun came out.

As he led his horse toward the adobe he saw the guitar player, and the two men who were at the bar loading two wagons. Around to the front, where he tied his horse as men on horseback, men walking, and pack animals moved south on the road. Walking in with his rifle in his left hand, he saw Paco there also. "Buenos dias," Paco said, "to you my friend, and to your rifle."

"Just might need it," Fran said. "It's better on long shots."

"You think someone might run off with your horse, senor?" Paco asked.

"He wouldn't get too far, Paco, now would he?" Fran answered.

Paco, smiling, said, "I'll get you some breakfast."

Fran watched as the men carried out furniture and things from other rooms. When Paco brought his breakfast, Fran asked him if he was leaving. "Si," he answered, "we leave for Monterey this very morning." Fran, looking puzzled, didn't have to ask. Paco telling him, "This is no place for us anymore. We moved the families weeks ago; now we go." Fran didn't say anything, but he knew these people, because of social pressure, were being forced away from their own lands.

"Maybe you could stay here, senor," Paco said. They wouldn't destroy it if you were here. Ah, but what am I saying? I don't think I can come back. But I will show you how to get in after we are done."

Taking Fran to the front door, Paco pointed out two of the pegs in the door. "Only these two, senor. See, the ropes pull them, and you raise the bar, and the door will open. The other door is the same; of course, if no one is here they will break the door."

"I'll come by and check, Paco, but I'm not going to be here very long either. I'm going back to the mountains."

"Then you, too, will look for gold," Paco said.

"No," Fran answered, "a friend is there, that I have to go back and see."

"I understand," Paco said, and he smiled as he said, "A beautiful young lady."

With a little chuckle Fran said, "No, an older man who I owe a lot; he led me, and some others all the way out here."

"A good friend is to be valued much," Paco said. "There are not many in a man's life."

"When you go back to the Sierra, how will you go?" he asked.

"Not by the river," Fran answered.

"Then you will go south to the pass near the Mission San Juan," Paco told him. "Come to Monterey for a visit, Franco. It is a little out of your way, but you will like it, I promise."

The sun was out now; having burned the fog away, his bedroll would be dry soon, and he could leave. "How much do I owe you, Paco?" Fran asked.

"Nothing, senor. Our talks were pay enough." Fran pulled out a small leather poke; and reached in with his thumb and forefinger. He brought out one of the nuggets he had separated from his other gold. "Here," he said. "Something you might want to give to your wife."

"She has been gone a long time, senor, but my daughter, who now cares for her brothers and sisters, yes, she would like this," Paco said. "She has sacrificed much taking care of the family, even marriage, and will soon be eighteen. Then they would say she was an old maid."

"Not at eighteen, I hope," Fran said.

"Oh, si, senor, girls marry young with my people."

Out in front, Fran rolled his bedroll and tied it behind his saddle, and they both watched the men passing.

"There must be hundreds of men. Where are they coming from?" Fran asked.

"Ships come in almost every day," Paco answered, "and not all I think are Americans; I guess they are the ones from other countries."

"They'll be crawling all over those mountains," Fran said absently.

"Si, senor, like ants on an anthill."

Fran looked at Paco for a second then said, "I think maybe more like maggots on a carcass, Paco."

"Aren't you being too harsh, my friend?" Paco asked.

"I don't think so," he answered.

They stood a few minutes longer, and Paco asked, "Will you come to Monterrey my friend?"

"I want to buy some clothes, and other things that shouldn't take too long, then, yes, I will stop by."

"Don't buy your things here; they charge too much. When you come to Monterrey, I will see you get some fine clothes," Paco said. Then he gave him a paper. "My name, senor. Ask anyone where I live; they will tell you."

Fran looked at the name on the paper, Paco Luna, and Paco said, "It's really Pablo Luna, but no one calls me Pablo anymore."

"Paco it will be," Fran said. "My name is Francis Leon, but they usually just call me Fran." Paco thought for a moment then said, "Your last name, senor? "Leon," Fran answered. "Your name means lion in my language," Paco said. Smiling, Fran said. "I have heard that, Paco, but until now I haven't really thought about it much. Then really whats in a name, should it mean something? "Only to people who believe in such things," Paco told him, "but some do, and they would expect something different from you." Well, please don't expect too much from me, Paco."

"I understand, my friend," Paco answered.

Fran mounted, and said, "We'll be seeing you Paco. I'll be there, but give me a couple weeks."

"Via con Dios, my friend. Don't make me wait too long."

He rode against the traffic, but it soon diminished, everyone evidently wanting to get an early start.

At the bank he took the two leather pouches out of his saddlebags, put his rifle on its sling, and walked into the bank. They didn't seem surprised, and he guessed it was because he was caring something into the bank, and not out of it.

"This way, sir," the young man said, and directed him to a chair where he could sit down. On the table in front of him sat a polished brass scale. Setting the pouches on the table, he sat down, his rifle across his lap.

An older man came to the table and introduced himself. "Thaddeus Davis," he said, "and you, sir?"

"Francis Leon," Fran answered.

"Glad to meet you," the banker said, and put out his hand, shaking his hand, and Fran knew this man had never worked at any kind of labor; his hand was as soft and smooth as a little child's.

Picking up the pouches, Mr. Davis said, "Oh, my, there's surely more than a day's work here."

"There is," Fran assured him.

"I hope you're not taking all this in cash, Mr. Leon."

"I would like some cash," Fran told him, "but I'll leave the rest with you."

Smiling broadly, Mr. Davis said, "Very good. I'll need your signature or mark but your signature if you intend to write drafts on your account." It didn't take long, and he had his cash, some drafts, and a deposit slip. He thanked Mr. Davis, picked up his rifle, and walked out to the front of the bank.

There were the things that he wanted to do, but right now he felt strange. He had cash but knew he wasn't rich or poor; he was solvent. He did feel he had an obligation to one man, but he knew that obligation could never be satisfied with anything monetary.

He got a bath, haircut, and shave, and bought some new clothes. They weren't the best, and he knew he'd paid a lot more than they were worth.

He knew he wasn't the only one who had brought in gold. It was obvious, as many of these men were celebrating in a grand style in this wide-open town. About anything a man could want was available, but all for a price.

The saloons and gambling houses, the most prevalent of all, and he felt it was the surest and fastest way for a man to be fleeced of everything he had.

Finding a hotel was easy, again not the best, but nice, with a dining room, bar, and a small gambling area that at present didn't interest him much. Asking the hotel clerk about a livery where he could leave his horse, he was told the one they recommended was on the street behind the hotel.

His horse stabled, he left his bedroll with his saddle and carried his rifle and saddlebags back to the hotel. The room, though small, was clean, but again, high priced.

Now he needed a place to stash the two pouches of gold he hadn't turned into cash. The water pitcher was large enough, and so was the chamber pot but were both probably too obvious. The building was new and hastily built; he tried the window and knew that as easy as it opened, there had to be sash weights, and the hollow area that held them. With some effort he soon had the cover board off, and his bags hidden away.

His extra clothes, though worn thin, he hung in the small closet, and the saddlebag he put over the foot of the bed. Then he checked everything so he would know when he returned if anything had been disturbed.

At the desk he asked the clerk if they had a safe; he would like to leave a bag of extra cash for safekeeping. After counting the cash, the clerk gave him a receipt, and he left, going into the dining room.

Looking at the menu, he was surprised at all the things they served. It had been a long time since he had tasted beef, so he settled on steak, but, looking at the price, he thought he might ask his waiter why he had to pay for the whole steer. But the waiter didn't set the prices, and an irritated waiter might slip when he served the soup.

The price was high, but the food was excellent, and the waitress that brought his dessert was pretty, her hair the color of a strawberry roan, freckles on her nose, slim, and an accent he couldn't place. He lingered over coffee when she smiled, then poured him another cup.

After paying his bill and leaving a nice tip, he went into the lobby, and sat down to read a paper he found there. He didn't know exactly how long he'd read, but it wasn't all that long till she was there. He knew her first name was Florence, from their meeting in the dining room, and she was beautiful, but that was all.

They talked, and she told him she lived in the hotel, as did some of the others who worked there. She wanted mostly to talk about him, like where he came from and how he came to be here. Some time elapsed before, she said, there were things she had to do in the dining room before retiring. He watched as she walked away, admiring a most attractive redheaded young woman.

He read more of the paper until running out of interesting articles. Leaving the paper, he hadn't realized the sun had gone down. Up in his room he washed with the cold water that was in the pitcher. He was standing with his shirt off, his pistol belt already hung on the bed's headboard, when he heard the light tapping. First he pulled his pistol, and then went to answer the door. With his pistol in his hand, his foot set so the door could only open a few inches. He opened the door cautiously. Surprised she was there, he stuffed the pistol down into his belt and opened the door a little more. She slipped quickly into the room, glanced back for a second, and closed the door. "Surprised?" she asked. He was, and said, "I am, but, welcome, please come in."

Chapter VI

She kissed him lightly and said, "They mustn't know; they wouldn't approve of this at all." She put her hands flat on his chest, emitting a slight hum, and said, "I like this," and lay her head on his chest.

Though neither tall nor large, Fran was a good average. There wasn't an ounce of excess on him to begin with, but the cutting of cordwood plus that long, hard ride. Then the moving of all that rock and gravel, had built him physically about as close to perfection as he would ever be.

Picking her up gently, he laid her on the bed, and blew out the kerosene lamp.

Waking to her stirring, he brought her to him again as she said, "I've got to go to work."

"In a minute," he said, kissing her into silence.

She got up, and said, "I'll see you at breakfast." Fran lay back and closed his eyes, falling back to sleep. The sun was up when he woke again, and he got up.

The cool water felt good, and he felt good but really hungry as he got into his clothes.

He had ordered his breakfast when she came to pour his coffee, and said, "Good morning, Mr. Leon." He had to smile when she asked, "Did you sleep well, sir?" and coyly said "thank you" when he answered, yes. Then she walked off to serve coffee to other patrons. Fran had to watch her; she was beautiful, he felt, and he wondered just where their relationship was going. He did have hopes, which left him vulnerable, and he knew he didn't want to be hurt.

After breakfast, when he felt he had lingered long enough, he left, walking down toward the waterfront. Passing the bank, Mr. Davis waved as he saw him walking by.

He watched the activity as boats were discharging their cargo. Tons of things were being off-loaded and hauled away; much of it, he knew, was heading up into the gold country.

Feeling there was somebody watching him, he walked on until he came to three wagons waiting in line to pick up their loads. Ducking under the heads of the last team and the back of the second wagon, he stopped. From here he could watch where he'd just come from.

The man, who he recognized, was fairly large. He'd seen him at the edge of the dining area in the hotel, near the bar and gambling tables. Now he wondered why this fellow had followed him, but he had no answer. It was not someone he knew, but he was sure he'd find out by just keeping his eyes open.

It was easy to lose him; he simply walked back the way he had come, but for part of the way, he walked through the maze of off-loading cargo wagons. Then going back to the road that led to the hotel, he went in through the lobby and up to his room. He found his things close to where they had been before but not exactly. The things in the closet had been moved, and not by the maid. The bed hadn't been made yet, and the water pitcher was empty.

Putting a chair under the doorknob just in case, he checked behind the board that covered the sash weight. Both the leather bags and their contents were there, undisturbed. He knew that if he had only gotten back a bit sooner he just might have been lucky or unlucky enough to have caught the culprit.

Everything put back, he went down to the lobby, and picked up another paper someone had left. Then he sat where he could look into the dining room. It was another copy of the same paper or the same paper; he didn't know. But it made no difference. He wasn't here to read anyway.

There was no sign of the man, and it made him wonder all the more. He stayed there until it was time for lunch. Now, in the dining room, he could see much better than from the lobby, but still there was no sign of the large man.

He ate his lunch, and again lingered over coffee. Few people were there for lunch, and they had a few minutes to talk. She said she needed to buy a couple of things, but with the price of things so high she was a little short. He made out a draft for a hundred dollars and handed it to her. She smiled faintly and thanked him then slipped the draft into the pocket on her apron.

A hot bath, a shave, his clothes washed, and he felt like a new man, all fresh and clean. Walking to the livery, he checked his horse just so it wouldn't forget him. Then talked to the hostler for a little while.

On the way back he bought a newspaper, and went into the lobby to read. Much of the news was about different areas where men were bringing gold out. Then there was a lot about the goings on in this infant city, plus all the crime that went on unpunished. He wondered how these people were letting these things happen, but felt sure that when they felt they had had enough they'd strike back.

She came again to the lobby to talk, but only for a few minutes, and he wondered if she would be there again this night. There was no commitment, one-way or the other.

Up in his room later, and in bed, he was looking up at the ceiling in the dim light from the street. He was thinking about before, and smiled; it had been wonderful. Dozing off, he thought he was dreaming when he heard the noise. Now awake, he was out of bed and at the door as he heard it again.

Opening the door just a little, he saw her there again. Just a little more and she slid through and into the room. It was then he realized he had nothing on, just his pistol in his hand. Even in the dim light he could see the smile on her face. Again he picked her up and carried her to the bed. "Is it funny?" he asked, and he was smiling now too.

They slept in each other's arms; morning came all too soon, and he had to let her go.

She smiled at him at his breakfast table, and again asked, "Did you sleep well, Mr. Leon?"

"Marvelously," he answered.

He was leaving the dining room, and turned to look back, not really knowing why. The same man was standing at the end of the bar, and talking to someone. It was someone he couldn't quite see standing in the doorway to the kitchen. Curious, he continued to look, and then she moved, and he knew.

Turning away, he was hurt, and confused but knew there was nothing he could do. Maybe there was a simple answer, but somehow he knew he was caught up in something where he could be the victim. "I guess I'd better be careful," he sighed, but he clamped his jaw tight, and was now determined he wouldn't go down easily. Whatever their game was he had a good hole card now but only because he realized all wasn't what it was supposed to be.

Up in his room he put everything in its place, and left; he would know if someone other than the maid had been there. But then maybe it was the maid who was doing more then she was supposed to.

Out of the hotel, he started his walk but stopped at a storefront to look in the window, and take a quick glance back. He was back there again but disappeared, and Fran walked on, thinking.

He remembered reading a story that told about how some people preyed on others. "I would be called the mark," he said to himself, "and she would be the shill. I guess that big guy is the kingpin. But how many others might there be, and what were their plans?"

Walking on, he kept checking, but the guy wasn't there or was keeping out of sight. Passing the bank, Mr. Davis greeted him again. Then he said, "Your account isn't going to last too long if you write those kinds of drafts," Mr. Leon.

He knew he had written only one, and it wasn't large at all. "Could I look at that draft," he asked. "I'm afraid I was under the weather when I wrote it, and I can't remember much." The draft was for a thousand, not a hundred, and it was so cleverly done that he would have honored it himself. *If she did this*, he thought, *she is sure no amateur.*

"Is there something wrong?" Mr. Davis asked as Fran continued looking at the draft. "No," Fran answered, but he did feel a little sick as things started adding up.

On down to the beach and the ships, he walked along thinking. The big guy wasn't following now, but maybe there was someone else; he couldn't tell.

Two men were selling some things, jewelry and some personal gear. The prices were decent, but there was nothing he really wanted except a telescope, leather case, and shoulder carrying case. He looked through the telescope, turning to check behind him, but saw no one who was looking his way. *It would be handy to have*, he thought, and he bought it. The man told him he was off a ship, and was selling some of his things so he could go and look for gold. "Good luck," Fran told him.

Always suspicious now, he walked with his right hand empty, and the hammer loop off his pistol. Now he walked a meandering route back to the livery stable, and had a few minutes of conversation with the hostler.

"You still hanging around this town?" the hostler asked.

"I'll be moving on pretty soon," Fran told him.

"Best thing," the hostler said, "You could get in trouble in this place; it's not good, it's bad."

"And you?"

The man smiled. "I ain't got nothing, and I'm too old for them to shanghi."

"To what?" Fran asked. And he told Fran how they could slip you some knockout drops in a drink. Then sell you to some captain who needs crewmen, and you're on your way to China maybe. "Good thing I'm not a drinker," Fran said. "Then stay out of dark alleys," the hostler went on, "they know how to use a sap too." Fran didn't know what a sap was, but figured what the outcome of an encounter like that would be.

He invited the hostler to lunch, and they went to a small restaurant where the older man said he ate now and then. "They serve good vittles," the hostler said, "at half the price of that hotel."

Fran found it was good, and a lot less than the hotel. They talked, and Fran told the hostler he thought he'd better head back to the mountains. "Don't want to lose a customer," the hostler said, "but the sooner you shuck this town the better."

"You planning look for more gold?" he asked.

"I don't know. I made a promise though, so it's back I go."

"That's the way it should be," the older man told him. "A man should keep his word."

After lunch he bought another paper, and read it in the lobby, but he had no visitor.

Up to his room he went, and he knew the room had been checked over again. After washing, he lay down and wondered if they'd seen him at the bank. He knew he was sure walking on thin ice; he could be in a lot of trouble at any time now.

Back down to the lobby, he'd read for a little while before supper. Again she didn't come into the lobby, and he was now real concerned.

At supper everything was cordial, but he knew something just wasn't quite right. Then he knew they could be playing a kind of a cat and mouse game with him. After supper and coffee, he went back into the lobby, and sat where he could look into the dining area again. There was nothing he might be suspicious of, but it was a no-show on her part. *It must be over,* he thought, and he went to his room. Before getting into bed he propped the chair under the doorknob, just little precaution. In bed he knew he would leave the next day. He missed her but knew it was going to have to be this way.

He was almost asleep before he heard it. With his pistol in his hand, and cocked, he moved the chair back from the door. If they tried to burst in, they'd get a surprise. But she was alone, and slipped into the room. Carefully he lowered the hammer on the pistol, bracing the door with the chair again.

Everything seemed the same, and he hoped his feelings wouldn't give him away. This night was as beautiful as the others; she was his, and he felt he might be wrong. It was everything a man could wish for and more, and he prayed he might be wrong.

She slept in his arms all night, and was there in the morning just as loving as she'd been before.

He closed the door behind her after she left, and he wanted it to be different, but he would go through with what he had planned.

Waking himself with the cool water, he readied his things but left the leather pouches behind the board. It was too early for him go down for breakfast, he paced the floor, now going over each step he had to take. The time passed slowly. He wanted it to start; he also knew he needed to calm himself. He was breathing way too fast, and was just too damn tense.

It was time, and he walked slowly down to the dining room, nodding as he said "good morning," to the desk clerk. He ordered breakfast, and smiling, she poured his coffee. He tried to smile as best as he could and hoped he didn't give himself away.

Eating slowly, he needed some time to pass; the bank had to be open when he got there. She poured another cup of coffee for him, smiling, and he watched her walk away. Now he wanted to be wrong. How could what they had be faked? Did he love her? He knew he did, and he wanted her to love him.

She poured his last cup, and then asked if he could spare another draft. Caught off balance, he hadn't figured on this happening. It came like a slap, and as something boiled up inside of him he retaliated. "The hen's eggs I had for breakfast were good," he said, "and I've already swallowed one goose egg. I don't need any more." His eyes glared into hers, and the muscles of his jaw pulsed as he kept clamping it closed. He wanted to some way hurt her now, just the way she was hurting him, but he didn't know how. Maybe what he'd just said did. The smile left her face, and the sparkle in her eyes faded. She was looking straight at him. Her face a mask, he could read nothing, and there was no expression whatsoever.

Turning, she walked away toward the kitchen. He drank his coffee slowly, but she never came back out.

Leaving the hotel, he was walking toward the bank when he saw him. He was standing in the door of a saloon that Fran would have to walk by going to the bank. Were they wise to what he had planned? He didn't know how they could be, but if they had guessed something, he would play their game until he saw a way out.

He stepped out when Fran approached. "We need to talk, Mr. Leon," he said. "I don't know what you'd want to talk to me about," Fran answered. "I don't know you."

"It's not about me," the man answered, "it's about your lady friend. Come in and have a friendly drink with me."

"I don't drink," Fran answered.

"One isn't going to hurt you, and this is important. You see, she owes some money," he said.

Inside, Fran walked to the closest table, passing another large fellow standing just inside. Sliding to the rear of the table, he sat with his back to the wall. Quite a few patrons were in the saloon already, and he figured they were probably those who usually drank their breakfast.

His host was still standing when he signaled the bartender then held up two fingers. Fran watched out of the corner of his eye as the bartender filled one glass on top of the bar with a bottle from the back bar. Then brought the second glass up from behind the bar.

That sure wasn't two drinks with the same ingredients, he knew, but how could he possibly tell which was which?

He brought them on a tray, and as he set the first glass in front of Fran. Fran slid it over in front his host, who was talking to the man behind him. The bartender started to say something but changed his mind when he saw the muzzle of Fran's pistol up over the edge of the table, pointed right at his middle.

The bartender walked away, and Fran watched as he put down the tray, took off his apron, and disappeared out the other end of the bar.

Turning around, his host said, "Drink up. This is just a friendly gesture on my part".." Fran just wet his lips with whatever was in the glass. "That's not the way, mate," his host said. "Like this," and he downed the whole glass that was in front of him.

Fran didn't. How could someone taste something drinking like that? Fran was still looking at him when he set the glass back down. He was looking at Fran when the blank look came over his face, and his eyes glazed. He was trying to sit when Fran holstered his pistol, and walked out around the table. Walking by the guy at the door, he said, "I think your friend is ill."

Out the door, he headed to the bank, and Mr. Davis. "I have to leave town," he told him, and could he divide what he had coming in two.

The banker insisted on counting everything to the penny but did hand Fran two canvas bags. Turning away from the hotel, he went through an alley to the street, and then to the livery.

He asked his friend if he would go to the restaurant, and get him something he could eat on the road. Then saddle his horse. "I've got to ride," he told him as he handed him the coins.

At the hotel he recovered the two leather bags, and balanced out his saddlebags.

Down to the desk he went, and he asked for his leather bag from their safe. And the desk clerk insisted the money had to be counted, and asked if he was checking out. Saying he had two days left, and insisted he take the money and sign the receipt.

The saddlebags were heavy, maybe a little lighter than when he came here, but not much. He glanced into the dining room as he left the hotel but didn't see her. And what good would it do anyway?

His horse was saddled, and a cotton flour sack was tied to the saddle horn. As he tied his saddlebags to the saddle, and his bedroll on, he talked to the hostler. He told him what had happened at the saloon, and the old man wanted to know what the fella looked like. When Fran told him, he told Fran he had better ride. "That's a bad bunch," the old man said. "You watch your back trail." He said, "I don't think they're going to let you get off if they can help it."

"Here's your change," the hostler said. "I took out the stable fee."

"Keep it," Fran said, "that information alone was worth it." He mounted, and the hostler handed him his rifle, saying, "You might need this, there's gonna be a lot a lot of varmints out there."

Chapter VII

The horse, rested wanted to move, and he let him trot but only until they hit the trail south with the others on it. Now he moved through the slower traffic. There were wagons, and even a few men walking. There was a rider ahead moving at about the same speed he was.

A few miles out he checked his back trail; there were a few other riders back there, but at this distance he wouldn't be able to identify anyone. He rode on another hour, and here the road rose slightly; from here he would have a good view of the trail behind him. At a small tree just off the trail he dismounted, thinking about that new toy he bought, and he took it out. Using the tree to steady his spyglass, he could check every person for a mile or two back. Eight riders were back there but only two that he recognized—the big guy that had stood by the door, and the bartender. Probably going to try to redeem himself, Fran thought.

Now he had to think, he could probably outride them. They didn't look like they were men used to the saddle or riding long distances; he was.

He got into the flour sack, taking out a sandwich, and ate a few bites; then he mounted, eating on the move. Before he'd taken the last bite, he knew what he had to do.

Out riding them would be easy enough, but that done, he would still always have to be concerned about his back trail. *Take care to the problem now and get it over with*, he thought.

He didn't know how far he had traveled, but he'd been moving fast. Seeing a trail that broke off to the west, he took it. The sign read Avenida de la Pulgas, he didn't know what that meant, and he really didn't care; the sun was descending, and would set in an hour or so. There just wasn't all that much time.

The trail steadily rose, so he knew he could easily be seen from the road below. It was a less traveled road and narrow, but could be traversed by a wagon. There were few places where one wagon could pass another, however. He rode a ways before he found a place suitable for what he knew he had to do. Rode his horse into some trees, where he tied him.

He walked back to the trail where he knew he'd have to wait. It shouldn't take much more than a half hour for them to get to where he was hidden.

Now, he hoped that no one had taken this trail before they did. There had been no Mexicans on the road, and there sure shouldn't be any miners coming this way.

They were riding side by side as they came toward him, both seeming to be confident in what they were doing, each a pistol on his hip, and a rifle in a saddle scabbard. They could probably use those pistols; but he wouldn't give them the slightest chance.

He wondered now, why didn't they think he just might wait instead of continuing to run? Too late now; they were there.

"Hold it right there," Fran said. "Try for your pistols now if you want, but you're dead men if you do." They were surprised. He figured they just didn't think he would stop. "Unbuckle your belts, and let them drop," he said. They did. "Now you, barkeep, ride your horse ahead a couple of lengths, turn him around, and dismount. Then walk on up the trail and wait."

"You do the same," he told the second man." That done, they stood in the trail together. As Fran was stepping away from the trees, he saw the doorman start to raise his arm. "Go ahead if you've got a gun up your sleeve, but at this distance you haven't got much of a chance," he told him.

"Now take off your shoes," he said. "You're not going to leave us barefoot," the bartender said. "I'll toss them in that brush; you can find them after I leave," Fran replied. The patch of brush was the same kind that Paco had told him to stay away from.

"Start walking," he told them. When they had gingerly walked far enough, Fran gathered up the pistols, hanging them over one of saddles. Picking up the shoes, he threw them into the brush. Mounted the horse without the pistol belts, and was about ready to ride, to retrieve his own mount. That's when the bartender hollered something at him. He rode closer and heard the man say, "She did a job on you, didn't she, Yank?" Fran knew the man was just trying to get him angry enough to come in closer. Then he heard the bartender say, "Ole Bo, and her got the same last name. You know Ole Bo; he's the one you slipped the Mickey to."

Fran rode away, switched to his horse, and led the other two horses down toward the main trail. Near dark, before coming to the trail, he threw everything but the rifles, pistols, and belts into another patch of brush, and turned their horses loose.

The trail was empty now; all the travelers had pulled off the trail, and were camped for the night. He rode on, thinking about what he'd heard. Bo had to be her brother, he told himself, but he knew in the back of his mind he was wrong.

After an hours ride in the dark, past camps, he came to a small stream, and let his horse drink. The expanse of yellowed grass on both sides of the stream was easily seen, even in the night. He led his horse out into it. Unsaddled, he put the horse on a picket, spread his bedroll, and lay down. Some fitful hours later, he fell into a deep sleep.

He woke to the sound of men, horses, mules, and a creaking wagon. It was past sunup, and he'd slept well past his usual waking hour.

Saddled up, he went to the stream, washed in the cool water, and both he and his horse drank before he mounted. Only sweet rolls were left in the flour sack; they were dried some now, but they would do. No fire, no coffee, only the branch water from his canteen; he'd make do with that, remembering tougher times. He rode on again past wagons, and men walking with their pack animals, not envious of them at all.

Riding now, he had time to think, and realized how little he knew about life. He was easily led, but only because he wanted so much for it to be true. Would he be hurt that way again? He vowed no. Could he be callous enough to protect himself? He didn't know; he loved life. There were sure to be other hard times, and difficult things for him to work through.

Touching his pistol, he knew he had the skill to take care of most any conflict involving arms. Some of the social skills that he felt he would need to survive through life, he realized he lacked. Even though he had just been given a harsh lesson, he didn't want to go through life alone. But how would he know how to recognize what he needed, from what he now feared the most?

He checked the pistols and rifles that he'd paid so dearly for. That goose egg had multiplied his draft tenfold. Neither pistol felt right, but he knew he could change that, as he did the pistol on his right hip.

They were both the same make and caliber, so it really made little difference. Rolling one in its belt, he stowed it in a saddlebag; then buckled on the other rig.

With the right-handled holster, the butt of the pistol faced forward. To draw it would require reaching across with his right hand. That was a much slower draw, but faster than reloading the pistol on his right hip, if he had exhausted its rounds.

He would devote hours of his time now; first he'd modify the holster, needing it to slant slightly forward. Then the grips on the pistol to fit comfortably into his hand and fingers. All of this now in preparing for what he felt might lie ahead. Just to give him a better feeling, plus the confidence he'd need, should he ever encounter more like the ones he'd just left in San Francisco.

But how could he prepare himself to be candid when confronting others? How could he keep from alienating honorable people he met, now that he would always be wary of their intentions. Would he have to learn on his own? That would be difficult. Then how many that could have been a friend, or that something else, might he lose? This would bother him for some time to come.

Staying away from the campsites of the traveling miners wasn't a problem right then. He didn't want to socialize right now anyway, and from the numerous times these areas had been camped in, they were some times even unpleasant to pass by.

Seeing smoke a ways off, he rode off the trail to a small group of adobes. The adults there were suspicious, but the children, though shy, did smile.

They didn't speak English but through some gestures he succeeded in acquiring a bowl of beans, and some of their tortillas.

He could see these people didn't have much, but other than being suspicious of him they seemed content. Hearing them talk, he picked out the word pistolero, and knew a man with two pistols would surely befit the name. He would learn later what their interpretation of the word meant, and would hear it many more times where Spanish was spoken. After he had eaten, he handed coins to the woman—the same amount he'd paid for his meal at the restaurant—and she shook her head. He wouldn't take the money when she tried to return it, and she ran off into their small adobe.

He had mounted, and was ready to ride off when she came back out with some things tied up in cornhusks. She handed them to him, said,

"Gracias senor. Via con Dios." Fran, nodding, said, "Thank you," and rode away.

The wagon trail split some miles below a mission, one trail continuing south and the other turning slightly to the west. He continued on the trail with the wagons, and pack trains but soon realized he was now heading in the wrong direction. He asked a man on horseback for directions to Monterey.

This trail, he was told, went through a pass into the valley below the Sierras. Pointing across the valley, he told Fran, "Head that way across the valley, and you'll run into the mission San Juan. If you push it, you can make it before sunset." Fran thanked the man and rode south across a pleasant valley.

He saw well-tended gardens as he neared the mission, and surrounding adobes. Someone must have alerted the padre; he was standing outside with two Mexicans dressed in loose white pants, and shirts.

"Welcome, senor," the padre said, as Fran rode up, surprising him. "To whom, and to what do we owe this pleasure," the padre went on. "Francis Leon, padre, and just a traveler going to Monterey to keep a promise."

"And the lion wears two guns."

"Yes, father, but only for protection," Fran answered.

"From who," the padre asked, "your own people or the Mexicans?"

"Neither." Fran answered. "So far it's only been foreigners, and so far I haven't had to shoot any of them, just ward them off."

"Step down, Senor Leon," the padre said. "We have but few Americans visit us. Most are anxious to get to the Sierras and gold."

Walking to a table and chairs on the veranda, he said, "Come, sit for a little while." Then he asked if he could stay the night. When Fran said," yes," he spoke to one of the young men. "He'll take care of your horse, and put your things in the room where you can spend the night. Don't concern yourself about your things. I am sure they will not be molested."

"Now," the padre asked, "who would you see in Monterey?"

"Pablo Luna," Fran answered." I know him well," the padre said. "He comes here to trade, but he hasn't been here for a while. Now, where did you meet him?"

"He and some other men had a small adobe just this side of the town you call Yerba Buena," he told the padre. "There isn't much there," the padre said. "There is now," Fran told him, "a lot of ships in the bay, buildings going up, and hundreds of people from all over the world. Just go look at the men traveling that trail on the other side of your valley."

The padre looked troubled, and Fran knew this invasion of people would mean problems for him, and everyone else here.

They were served slices of melon, fruit, and grapes. The padre saying he liked to eat light at his evening meals, and this time of year was especially good for that.

After eating, the padre walked, showing Fran some of the mission, and where his room was. Then they went to the adobe houses, where there were lanterns burning, music, and people dancing. "We rest during the heat of the day," the padre told Fran, "then celebrate the day in the evening."

"I could get used to that," Fran said. "I never did like working on hot afternoons."

The night air was still warm when Fran retired, but his room was cool in the adobe building. He fell asleep listening to the music of some far-off guitarist.

Up before the sun, he dressed, and walked outside into the dark. The sun would be up soon, and the temperature would change rapidly once it appeared. He was walking along the veranda when the padre surprised him, sitting at a little table in the dark. "Didn't see you, padre," Fran said. "Sit down," the padre said. The sunsets are beautiful, but we will see the birth of a new day.

The dark sky started turning a lighter blue as Fran watched. The first bright orange light peeked over the mountain, and the orange rays of light flashed across the sky above them. "I've never seen a day break like that before, padre," Fran said. "It doesn't happen every day like that," the Padre said, "only occasionally, but I am rewarded by being here when it does. "I guess I was lucky then," Fran said, "or did you order it for me?" "If I only could," the padre answered, smiling.

They ate their breakfast of eggs, meat rubbed with chili, tortillas and chocolate. The padre pointed to a road leading off toward the southwest. "That's the coach road that leads over the hills, and to another valley. It's a little steep maybe for a coach, but easily passable for a man on horseback.

"Follow it southwest across the valley. You will come to an opening through the hills there. It's called the Arroyo Seco. Follow that road; it will take you straight to Monterrey."

"But after Monterrey where does the lion go?" the padre asked. "Back to the mountains and a good friend who's waiting there."

"Then you've been to the Sierra," the padre said.

"Came over those mountains from the east with five others," Fran told him. "All the way across the country on horseback."

The padre was smiling when he asked, "Will you come back this way?"

"Almost have to," Fran answered.

"Then you must stop," the padre said. "You must have some things to say about that journey."

"Not too much," Fran answered, "other than there's some harsh country that has to be crossed."

As Fran stood, the padre said, "You tell Pablo that Father Anthony sends his blessing."

"That I can do," Fran answered. His horse already saddled, all he had to do was load his saddlebags, bedroll, and rifle.

Walking his horse back to where the padre stood at the mission, Fran said, "Thank you, Father Anthony. I enjoyed your hospitality." A gold coin from his pouch he gave to the padre, and a silver coin to each of the young men who stood by him. "You don't have to do this," the padre said."

"But I do," Fran said. "It's a must on my part." Mounting, he said, "See you, padre."

"Via con Dios," they all answered.

The coach road was steep but only for a short distance, and he was soon on top; the valley on the other side, lush and cool. The slope going down was easy, and the breeze coming from the west had a faint smell of the sea, and its salty water.

There were a few adobes here and there with their gardens, and then a group of adobes in a small settlement. He drew the stares of some of the people, and he knew it was because of the two pistols.

The streambed he came to, was mostly dry, only pools of water at a few places, but dry sand for yards in between. Crossing the streambed where it was dry, he continued on until he came to the wagon trail, that paralleled the rolling, grassy hills. It was markedly warmer here, the hills blocking the breeze that moved through the flat valley. The trail led more toward the south here before turning to the west and into the hills. Then it followed along a stream, and in places twenty to thirty feet, above the rocky streambed. The trail itself fairly level, was an easy ride. Large oak trees, and grass, and those little grouse seemed to be were everywhere.

He bathed in the cool water, and washed clothes while his horse grazed. The rabbits here were small, and he thought they were real young, but all he saw were close to the same size. An hour later he was roasting two of them over his fire. They were excellent eating, and he relaxed on a dry sandy spot, until he felt it was too late to think about traveling on.

He moved his horse to another spot, and rolled out his bed. He felt good at this place. He lay on his back, and looking up at the sky, watched the stars wink on, one after another. Alone, he was lonesome but satisfied he'd made it through, what was now only a mental scar; that he hoped would heal.

Chapter VIII

It was still dark when he awoke. All was quiet except for the sound of the water, and his horse cropping grass. The sky was still dark, and he lay back, watching for shooting stars. When the sky started to lighten, he got up. The sunrise here would be as at the mission, and it would be full light before the sun would shine into this canyon.

It was cool now as he rode, but he figured it would get hot once the sunlight poured in. But it didn't. Before it could get really warm, he broke out of the hills and onto flatter ground. The breeze was now coming out of the west, from the ocean, and now with a heavy scent of salt, and seaweed.

He went south, and west now, across sandy ground, brush, and long salt grass. It was over an hour before he saw the mission, and the town around it. Then the view of blue water to the west, that ran unbroken out to the horizon.

There were ships at anchor here too but only a dozen or so, nothing like the bay at Yerba Buena. There were people on the road now as he neared the adobes. Most looking dubiously at him but some with a jaundiced eye, and he knew again it was the two pistols. Unbuckling his second sidearm, he reattached the buckle backwards, and hung it over the saddle horn. Somewhat out of sight, but he still had the other pistol; that was visible.

Their suspicions he knew were justified he saw no man riding or walking, armed with a rifle or pistol. Would this pastoral scene continue here? He didn't see how it could with what was happening just a few days ride north.

Asking about Paco, Fran simply said his name, "Pablo Luna," and the person would point the way. Three times he asked, the last man pointing to the store a few doors away. Tying his horse in front, he took his second pistol off the saddle horn, hanging it off his left shoulder as he walked in.

Paco and another man were busy with other people that he figured were customers.

He was looking at some of the things in the store when he heard a girl's voice that sounded somewhat irritating to him. "Papa," she said, and then added something in Spanish that he didn't understand. Turning around, he stood face to face with the girl. No a young woman, dressed in black riding clothes, flat Spanish hat, boots, and all. With light, cream-colored skin, raven hair, and the bluest eyes he'd ever seen.

He was looking into those eyes when she spoke, but he didn't understand a word of it except senor, even though he knew she was speaking to him.

Paco walked by and said, "Oh, I see you've met my daughter. You go on talking; I'll be back in a minute."

"I'm sorry," Fran said, but I don't understand Spanish. In English now, she said, "I just asked why you were looking at me the way you were."

"I wasn't looking at you; at first, I was looking at merchandise," he said. "But now I see blue eyes."

"I have my mother to thank for them," she said, "and I'm sorry that I thought you were staring."

"I didn't mean to be impolite," she went on. "I just didn't understand, but I'm glad that my eyes have impressed you, somewhat."

Paco was back with a quirt, and handed it to his daughter. "Thank you, Papa," she said.

"But do you need the latigo?" her father asked.

"My horse," she said, "he's refused twice at the fence." Fran had heard that Mexicans, like others, could be rather cruel with their animals.

"Shall we go watch?" Paco asked Fran.

"I'd like that," Fran answered. They followed, Fran only taking long enough to untie his horse, and bring him a long.

They watched as she brought the horse around to the gate, and he shied away, not wanting to jump. The girl raised the quirt, and was ready to whip the horse. Fran couldn't help himself when he hollered, "No don't do that." She turned toward him, a frown now on her face, but did lower that whip. She was looking at him rather coolly now, with those blue eyes.

"I'm sorry," he said, "but maybe I can help." Fran tied his horse, and went over the fence. He walked to the practice gate she wanted the horse to jump and, lifting one end, moved it until the shadow behind it disappeared. "Try it again," he told her.

She rode the horse around the arena trotting him, tried him on the gate and he cleared it, easily. Moving the gate back to it former position, Fran motioned her to bring the horse to where he was. Holding the bridle, he led the horse to the back of the gate. The animal lowered his head before he would move through the shadow, now behind the gate. They went back through the shadow again, and, looking up into those blue eyes, he asked, "Would you try him again?" The horse easily cleared the gate with out a problem. Fran was on the outside of the fence when she looked back at him, expressionless.

"I'm afraid I've made two bad impressions on your daughter, Paco, and I really haven't met her," Fran said. "Oh, pardon, my friend, "Paco said, "but I thought you were carrying on a conversation when I walked by. I am sorry, but don't you worry, I'm sure my daughter will not judge you harshly."

"I hope not," Fran answered. "I really meant no harm."

"But how did you know why the horse didn't want to jump the barrier?" Paco asked.

"I think the horse saw it just as I did. From this side of the gate, its shadow looked like there was another gate lying flat on the ground. Seeing it that way, he felt it was a jump he couldn't make. The quirt would have done nothing but hurt the animal."

"You have feelings for animals, my friend," Paco said.

"I guess," Fran answered. "You see I've never seen an animal beaten into submission, that was a better animal because of it."

"This horse of mine, Paco, has balked a lot of times, and saved me from things I didn't see, especially at night. He's not a fine bred animal like your daughter's, but he has good survival instincts, so I take care of him, and he takes care of me."

"I bought her that horse," Paco told Fran, "because she has done much keeping our family together after we lost her mother. She deserved the best I could buy; now maybe she can enjoy life after the years she worked caring for her brothers and sisters."

"That's a fine horse, Paco. He will give her years of pleasure, I'm sure."

They were almost back to Paco's store when she rode her horse in front of them. Dismounting, she said, "I'm sorry, senor, but I think we've come together you might say out of step." Fran, smiling, said, "It's, 'on the wrong foot.'"

"Oh, yes," she answered, smiling.

Putting out her hand, she said, "I'm Angela Luna."

Fran, taking her hand, said, "Francis Leon."

"It's my fault," Paco said, "but I thought ..."

"It's all right, Papa," she said, breaking in. "Everything is fine now. You just make sure Senor Leon comes to our house this evening."

Mounting, she smiled, and nodding slightly, said, "Senor," and rode away. Fran looked after her as she rode, thinking how beautiful she was.

Paco brought him out of his train of thought when he said, "I have a place where you can stay. We should go there now and put your horse to rest." They walked in the same direction she had gone. "It's my sister's home," Paco told him. "She stays with us now since her husband passed away. She has helped Angela, giving her the chance to be a young girl for a while."

The houses were actually next to each other except for the gardens between them. Every house had a garden; each household plot seeming to take care of most, if not all of their own needs. Many had chickens, goats, or a cow. Paco's sister's house had a barn and pasture, but there was no stock there now except a few chickens that were wild. Later he was told they were some of the fighting chickens that his brother-in-law raised. "We come and look for their eggs," Paco said, "but they hide them so good, sometimes we can't find them, and they raise a few more."

His horse out in the pasture and his things in the house, Paco insisted they go to the cantina. "A bite to eat, a cerveza, and then we will rest for a few hours," he said.

Paco asked about his trip down, and Fran told him about following the men heading for the Sierras, too far. "I left the trail near the mission San Juan," Fran said. "A little out of the way," Paco said, "but no matter; you are here."

"The padre there, Father Anthony, sends his blessing," Fran told him.

"I haven't seen the padre for a while." Paco told Fran. "I should go there again soon; I haven't been there to trade for some time now."

I met my Rosemary near there, and we were married at the mission," he told Fran. "Many sweet memories from there, but some bitter ones too.

"You see, I am a mestizo," Paco said.

"You'll have to explain, Paco. I've never heard the word before."

"I'm what your people call a half-breed. My mother was an Indian; her people worked at the mission, and the ranchos near there. My father was from Mexico City, a trader who I didn't get to see very often, but he always brought us nice things when he did come. My uncles were the ones who taught me how to work and ride.

"I was about thirteen or fourteen when we heard my father and his mule train disappeared from Santa Fe, and we never heard a word after that.

"I could ride well and went to work as a vaquero for a ranch close by, and soon worked my way up to their best. I loved the work, but I'm afraid I was like every other vaquero; we treated the horses poorly—Spanish spade bits, large spurs, and whips. We rode two or three horses until they could run no more, some days. I made sure I was the best, and the Patron always rewarded the best, so I wore nice clothes and had beautiful silk bandanas for my hat and neck.

"There was a big fiesta just for the people who came to visit. I saw that pretty girl but only from a distance until after the rodeo. I had won many of the events, and she was to present our prizes. I rode up and stopped; she said something and gave me my prize, but I heard nothing. I was looking into those eyes until someone behind me slapped the horse I was riding, and told me to get out of the way.

"I learned from her mother later that she had turned to her father and said, 'That's the man I'm going to marry.' We did get married, to the disappointment of some. But her parents knew if they didn't let us get married in the church, we would have run away.

"I was told to leave that rancho by the Patron; he wanted her to marry this old friend of his.

"We went to the mission then. I worked, and she taught English, insisting that I learn too. I learned to read, write, and handle money. But we were poor except for what her parents left her before going back to Spain. Our love was all we really had, but that was everything; we were lovers, morning, noon, and night. And we were so happy because of the love and passion that filled our lives; we felt it was everything.

"She told me one day we had to move to Monterey. We went to the padre who was there then, and he said, 'Yes, you should go. You can trade with the Boston men, you speak their language.' He gave us his blessing, and we came here.

"Our first place here wasn't very big, of course. We were only two then. We worked, lived, and ate here. The ship captains paid me to find the hides and tallow they would need when they went back, and the ranchos paid me to sell their hides and tallow. The store then was just a warehouse, but with the things that came in off the ships we bought more, and we grew. Now I trade here and anyplace I care to.

"You see, Franco, she was not only beautiful, but she was intelligent. I don't know what would have happened to me if she hadn't found me."

"You would probably still be a vaquero on that rancho," Fran said. How about that Patron who fired you, Paco? You ever see him?"

"Oh, si. I worked with his hides, and he apologized. Said he was sorry he meddled in someone else's life. Then one of the vaqueros I rode with back then, brought a fine mare from that rancho, telling us it was a present from his Patron.

"You see, I never held any bad feeling. I would not be here today if he didn't send me away then. I have so much, so much more than when I rode there. There are no regrets. Now see, I have so much more than most.

"But come now, its time for a short rest, and tonight we will celebrate."

He left Fran at the little adobe, saying he would have someone call when it was time for a bite to eat, adding, "Then we can enjoy the evening."

He dozed off for a while, and the boy that came and woke him had the same color eyes as his older sister, but they didn't seem to look into your very being like hers did. "Papa said he'd meet you on the veranda," the boy told him. His eyes did sparkle, though, and there was surely mischief there. "Thank you," Fran said, and the boy scampered off.

The sun had disappeared into the ocean; only a few orange wispy clouds showed where it had gone. Paco sat at a small table with a decanter, and glasses on the table. "Vino?" Paco asked as Fran sat down. "Thank you, Paco" Fran answered. "I'm not one for drink."

"You'll like this," he said. "It's a special wine flavored by a sea voyage."

"I'm afraid I might like it," Fran said, "and I've seen what drink does to men."

"This is not a wine to drink that way; it's to enjoy for its flavor, and one glass sipped slowly will not bother you," he said as he poured. Fran did sip it a bit at a time, and told his host it was good.

Crisp tortillas, salsa, bits of cheese, and sausage that was pepper hot; she brought them, then sat next to Fran. "Would you walk to the plaza with me, after?" she asked. "I'd like to see the dancing and listen to the music." Fran was surprised, but he was able to answer with a," yes, of course."

As it grew dark, lanterns were lit here and there, some close by, then many more toward the plaza, and then the music began.

Paco walked with them but left when they came to the cantina. "You go ahead. I've got some things to take care of," he said.

She had his hand in hers, and held it tight. "You didn't wear your pistol," she said. "I thought you could protect me," Fran told her. "I would try," she answered. He felt the people's eyes on them, and wondered. She talked to a few people, but he didn't understand what was said. Finding a bench, they sat down, and she moved close. He could feel her warmth, and it was bothering him. He moved a little, and she asked, "Is there something wrong?"

"Yes," he answered.

"Shall we leave?"

"*No*," he replied.

She was looking at him with a smile on her face. "Do I bother you that much?" she asked. Looking back at her, he said, "Yes."

"I'm glad," she said, and squeezed his hand tighter.

They watched for quite a while before she said, "I think we'd better go." Walking slowly, Fran took his hand out of hers, putting it around her back as they walked.

"Did my father tell you about my mother?" she asked. "He did," Fran, answered. "They loved each other very much."

"They did," she answered. "He still does, and also loves to tell people about her. I think if it wasn't for us he would have soon followed her."

"What are you going to do tomorrow?" she asked. "I'd like to see about some decent clothes," he said. "They can wait," she told him. "In the morning we should take the horses and go for a ride on the beach. "Sounds like fun," he answered.

At the door she turned, gave him a quick kiss, and went in. He stood for a second, and the door opened a little. She looked out coyly and said, "Good night, Francis."

He thought about her most of the night. In the morning he went out in the pasture to check his horse. The horse was lonesome, he knew, when it came running to him. He took a quick bath in the trough with the horse looking on. "I'll be back after breakfast," he said to the horse, just as if he understood. Then, standing in front of the animal, he told him, "I wish you could talk; maybe you could help me figure things out. I'm sure you wouldn't give any poor advice." The horse just stood looking at him. "You think I'm crazy, talking to a horse, don't you?" Then he had to laugh at himself. He loved her, he knew, but didn't know what to do. "I need her but don't know how to tell her, plus I'm afraid."

The little brother was there again, grinning from ear to ear, and said, "Angela has your breakfast," and ran off giggling. "You think it's funny," Fran shouted after him, but he had to smile.

She was waiting on the veranda. "Would you like breakfast here or inside?"

"Here would be fine," he said, "and your father."

"He's gone to the graveyard at the church; he goes there when he has things to think about, but he said he would see you later, Francis."

They ate together, both now wondering but remaining silent until they had finished, and she had cleared the table. Back outside, she sat for only a minute, and then asked, "Do we ride?"

"We ride," he answered.

"I must change," she said. "I'll meet you here in a few minutes."

His horse came to him as soon as he stepped into the pasture. "Ready to go, are you?" Then he realized he was talking to the horse again, as usual. "Anyone hears me talking to you will think I've gone a little off the trail," he said.

She was there waiting as he walked up. "What took you so long?" she asked, smiling. "I needed some advice from my horse," Fran answered, knowing she'd think he was kidding. Riding side by side toward the beach, he tried not to keep looking at her, but found it all too pleasurable. He would get caught, but looking at her did make him feel good, and happy. He was glad he came here, but now he wondered if this wasn't the ulterior motive behind Paco's inviting him. If it were the reason, then he would surely have to thank him.

They had only ridden a short distance when Fran, reining his horse to a stop, asked, "Have you talked to your horse?" Stopped alongside him now, she answered, "No. Why?" with a somewhat puzzled look. "Because right now he's telling you some thing," he told her. Both of their horses stood with the ears forward, looking toward the closest grassy dune. Now she was looking in that direction. "Is there something there?" she asked, just as a young man stood up, tucking in his shirt; then a young girl stood, straightening her blouse. "Oh, my," she said, as she urged her horse forward.

Waving at the young couple, Fran said, "Pardon us," and rode after her. Alongside her again, he was smiling. She looked at him, but she wasn't smiling as she asked, "Do you think we disturbed them?"

"I'm afraid we did." Fran answered.

"Oh," she said. "Oh, how terrible," she added. Then, shaking her head, she looked at Fran and laughed, urging her horse faster.

Riding up through the dunes, they rode to the low hills behind them. Fran tied the horses, and then sat down, looking out over the dunes to the sea. "Do you care for me Francis?" she asked. "I'm afraid I might love you," he answered.

"Don't be afraid. I'll never hurt you."

"Guess I'd better ask your father, but I have a hunch he's already had it planned."

For the first time he held her close, and kissed her like he'd been wanting to.

Riding back they saw her father sitting on the veranda. They put up her horse, and then she rode behind him past Paco to put his horse in the pasture. As they walked up Paco, smiling, asked if they had a good time.

"Are you drinking before lunch, Papa?" Angela asked, seeing the decanter, and a glass on the table. "No," her father answered. "I was just waiting to see if I might have something to celebrate."

"You're a schemer, Paco," Fran said. "You had an ulterior motive when you invited me for a visit.

"Are you sorry you came, Francis?"

Fran, smiling, asked, "Are you going to let me marry her?"

"Si," Paco told him. "I knew it would happen; she told me. You sit now."

Paco went inside but came right back out with two more glasses. Filling all three glasses, he said, "We drink to your happiness." Then holding his glass up, he said, "My blessing, Francis, Angela. I'm happy now." There were tears in his eyes, and Angela, putting her arms around her father, said, "Gracias, Papa. One day you must tell me how she told you."

Angela went inside, and in a few minutes came back out with her Aunt Maria, another glass, and lunch. Maria, holding her glass up, said one word, "Amore."

They ate, and drank the wine. Paco told them, the bottle must be empty before we leave the table." Fran thought the wine was excellent, and he told Paco, "Like life when things are right." Paco answered, "Warm, mellow, and sweet."

Maria, clearing the table, went inside. "Time for siesta," Paco said, and followed Maria. Angela, taking Fran's hand, led him to the little adobe.

He woke in the waning light as she still slept, as perfect as any person could be. She was flawless he saw, as he touched her lightly. Waking, she pulled him to her, saying, "Rest, Mio Franco."

CHAPTER IX

When he woke again, there was a fire burning in the fireplace, and he could smell something cooking. He moved as she told him, "Get up. Breakfast is almost ready. We've got to keep you strength up, you know."

They ate without dressing, and she told him, "There's water warming for a bath."

"Do I get my back washed?" he asked, smiling.

"Only if you wash mine first," she answered.

Walking hand in hand to the tailor's, Angela asked, "how long before they would leave for the Sierra." "How can I take you there without a house?" Fran said. "I don't care about a house. I can live in a hut, like my mother did, but I will be with you, Francis. We're one now." He smiled, and said, "We can stop at the mission and have Father Anthony marry us."

"I'd like that," she answered. "That's where they were married; it will make Papa happy too."

Brown was the color Fran picked for his vaquero-style pants. "They're so dull," Angela said. "But a smudge of dirt isn't going to be so obvious, is it? "But you can go ahead, and pick out what you'd like me to wear, when we get married if you like," he said"

She was speaking Spanish, ordering the things they wanted, as Fran busied himself looking at some of the hats, and other things in the shop.

Leaving, she told him they could get their hats, and shirts at her father's store. "We're going to need a packhorse," Fran said. "My horse can't carry much more then I already have."

"Papa will know where to buy a horse, but there are other things too."

At the adobe, in bed, they made out the list, talking and laughing, as they each thought of some personal things they would certainly need. But there was an occasional interruption, for something at that time they felt was more important.

At the wedding meal, Angela asked her father to tell her how her mother had told him about Francis.

"I'd gone there to start another store because I thought there would be one needed, and there was. But I was wrong to think these were Americos like the Boston men. Those gringos there hated all the Mexican people, and those who lived at Yerb Buena had to leave or one day be killed. There were only a few left who would trade with us, so we were packing to leave too."

"Then Franco came to the cantina, he asked politely about buying a meal, and we talked. He treated me like a gentleman, with respect, demanding nothing, like the others had."

"That night I asked your mother about him. Why was he like he was, and should I feel he would be a true friend?"

"Franco was there for breakfast the next morning, and we talked again. He saw we were packing to leave, and understood why. He wanted to pay for the meals, but it was just the food we had, and I told him no, that I felt our talks were worth more than the food."

"When he gave me the piece of gold, it felt warm." He said, "something for your wife. I told him that she was gone, but I had a daughter that had sacrificed much to take care of my other children. He told to give it to you."

"I knew then she had given me that sign. He had to come to Monterey, and when he saw you he would fall in love with you, the same way I did with her. It was from that piece of gold that I felt her warmth, and I knew."

"Oh, Papa," Angela said." I love your story; it was beautiful." She hugged and kissed his check.

"Go now," he said. "It's time for siesta."

She was crying as they walked to the adobe, and, inside, Fran held her while she composed herself.

"My father believes in many of the old ways of his mother."

"Do you feel he could be wrong?" Fran asked.

"No," she answered, holding him tightly. "I believe he's right, because how else would he have known to bring you here?"

"Do you think we have the love they had?" Fran asked.

"I don't know," she answered, "but I want what they had and all the love we can have forever."

With their plans, all made, and their list completed, they could really rest this siesta. Tomorrow would be a busy day.

Paco was sitting at the table in the morning, and asked what they had planned for the day. "I thought I'd show her how to use a pistol," Fran said. "It's something she needs to know; where we're going, there are some bad people. Then we have to pick up some things before going to the tailor's."

"What's on your list?" Paco asked.

"I have the list, Papa," Angela said.

"Let me see," her father said. "Maybe I can find some of these things for you." He took the list, looked at it for a few seconds, and then, folding it, put it in his pocket.

They had breakfast with Paco then rode out to the beach and sand dunes. There were no surprises this day, the young couple having probably found a more secluded spot for their romantic sojourns. They did smile when they passed that spot, though.

The pistol was large for Angela's hands, but with both hands Fran knew she could manage. "With both hands," he said, "just point straight at the center of what you want to hit." After only a few shots she had no trouble hitting the two-foot circle he drew on the side of the dune. Now all she had to do was get used to the weight of the pistol on her hip. He did some work on the belt, punching holes so the belt would fit.

Then they went to the tailor shop, where Fran got a surprise. There were four pairs of pants, all the same color—brown.

"I thought you didn't care for that color," Fran said.

"I really don't," she answered, "but I realized you were right. This isn't going to be an overnight trip, and I'd like to be dressed like you."

"Two pairs of riding breeches, and boleros to match. "We'll be dressed like twins," Fran said.

"I hope you don't start treating me like a sister then," she said.

"That's never going to happen," he answered. Handing her his coin pouch, he said, "Take what you need; there should be enough there."

He carried the packages out to the horses, tying them behind his saddle. She had a serious look on her face when she came out of the shop.

"There's a lot more there than I needed," she said. "Shouldn't you leave some at home?"

"Home has been that saddle for me most of the time since I left the mountains," Fran answered.

At the adobe, Angela carried some of their things to the door, opened it, and stood looking in. With the rest of the packages Fran walked up, and they both stood, looking at the sacks, and boxes piled in the middle of the floor.

"What is all that?" Fran said.

"I think it's what my father bought us for the trip," Angela said, "but it's obvious he's added some things."

Letting his horse out into the pasture, Fran looked at two others that were there now in the barn. There were two packsaddles and bags; now he knew Paco intended for them to take some other things, and he wondered what they could possibly be.

Angela's horse taken care of, they went to the table on the veranda and her father.

"Have you seen?" Paco asked.

"If you're talking about all those things on the floor, and the second packhorse, we have," Fran answered. "But it's more then we need for the trip." "And with winter coming you're going to survive eating rabbits and deer."

"No," Paco said. "You need other things; eating just meat you can get sick,"

"Charley told us about trappers in the Rockies who sometimes got sick from that." Fran said.

"Sailors get that sickness too," Paco said. "They call it scurvy. It's not a pretty word. Besides the food, there's seed for you to plant that will help you too."

"There's a lot for two packhorses, I know, but you can carry some on your horses, in your saddlebags," Paco said.

Fran sat for a minute then said, "I'll be right back."

Paco looked at his daughter. She shrugged and said, "I don't know, Papa."

Back at the table, Fran lifted the bags off his shoulder and set them on the table with a thump. Opening each saddlebag, he took out two soft leather bags from each. He put back the two that held the smallest amount in them, and then he slid the two heavy bags over in front of Paco. "No need hauling all that any farther,' Fran told him.

Paco, sitting, hefted one of the bags then quickly undid the thongs that held their tops. Opening both bags, he exclaimed, "You carried all this from the Sierras?"

"I changed some into coins at Yerba Buena, but there was no reason to change all of it. I only changed into coin what I needed."

Hefting each bag, Paco asked, "How much?"

"About twenty pounds in each bag."

Paco thought for a minute. "Close to six thousand dollars, Francis," he said.

Angela, on her feet, looked into the bag. "Are you rich, Francis?" she asked.

"Not quite," he answered, "but it could be a good start."

She sat back down, holding her head in her hands. He knelt beside her chair, saying, "It's all right." Afraid she didn't like what she saw, he told her, "I'll give it away."

"No," she answered. "It's just the way you surprised me. First I see you as a pistolero and wondered."

"Now," she laughed, "I find you carry around thousands of dollars in your saddlebags, like a bunch of soiled socks."

"I'm sorry,' he said. "I just didn't have any other place to put it."

"There's been some gold brought here," Paco told Fran, "and I know two men who would buy it. But I think sending it back with one of the ships would be better; that's what would happen to it anyway."

'Franco," Paco asked, "What is it you want to do?"

"Were going to the Sierra," Fran said. "Charley's still waiting there I'm sure. There's good pasture; we'll build our cabin. Then I don't know, maybe farm some, I guess."

"Think about a store," Paco said, "those men up there are going to need supplies."

"Your brother should be home tomorrow," Paco told his daughter, "and I'll bring your sisters home from the convent for a few days, so you can see them before you leave. Now I'd better put these away." Taking the bags, he went into the house.

Angela helped her aunt with the meal, and then she and Fran retired to the adobe for siesta. "How big will the cabin be?" she asked.

"Just one small room; there's not going to be enough time for much more. We can add on later," he said.

"For now, we don't need any more room, but some day," Angela said.

Awakened by the rumbling noise outside, Angela hurried to get dressed. "Pepe's home," she said. Fran, up now, dressed hurriedly, and they both went out.

Paco was on the veranda talking to a horseman. The rider, turning as they approached, said, "I'll be back in a few minutes," and he rode after the line of pack mules that were filing past. Paco, sitting down, said, "He'll be back in a half hour; they'll drop everything off at the warehouse, and then straighten things up in the morning."

Maria, awake now too, brought fresh fruit, and grapes, putting them on the table. "They ride through town, and wake up the dead. Why don't they stop for siesta?"

"They would have had to unload all the mules and horses, and then take care of them."" Then, they would have been late and missed fiesta," Paco said.

He came walking toward them, a cloud of dust around him as he brushed the dust off his clothes. He was dressed like a vaquero minus the spurs. He was young, and slim, tanned by the sun, but his blue eyes branded him as one of the Luna children. He flopped into a chair, and began eating grapes, after handing his father some folded papers.

"And who is this, big sister, you're sitting so close to," Pepe asked.

"If you would shut up for a minute, I'll introduce you, little brother," Angela answered.

"This is Francis Leon. Francis, my brother Pepe."

Fran had to smile at Pepe as he shook his hand. Like his little brother Michael, Fran could see Pepe was enjoying life.

"Do I see an extra sparkle in your eyes, sister," Pepe asked.

"And if you do, little brother?" she asked.

"Then it's congratulations, senor Leon; you take a fair rose from our garden, but we will talk again later. Right now I need a warm bath, and some rest. I don't want to miss fiesta."

Paco, looking after his son, said, "I'll have a talk with him, Angela."

"It's all right, Papa," Angela answered, "and Pepe is just being Pepe. He's still a young boy, but he's doing a man's work; he needs his fun."

"But he acts kind of loco sometimes," Paco said.

"He's living, Papa. He loves to dance and everyone loves him because of it."

Back at the little adobe where they'd try to rest a little, Angela was telling Fran, "We have to go to fiesta tonight. Pepe and the others who work with him will be there to dance. I promise you'll enjoy every minute."

Maria and Angela were setting their supper table when Pepe came in all dressed for the night—vaquero clothes with fancy boots, and a bright scarf.

"I want to leave early, he said.

"Maybe you could stay and eat with us," Paco told him, "then have a drink to celebrate."

"Remember, Papa," Pepe said smiling," the one who dances with a full belly dances like a clumsy jackass. Then could I expect a kiss good night from a pretty senorita, with wine on my breath? No, Papa, this is our first night back, and I want it to be a real fiesta."

"You have to excuse your papa, Pepe," his father told him. "You know I can see now what I missed, but maybe one day, who knows. Now you go and dance like she taught you, and kiss a young lady for me."

"Papa," Angela exclaimed, "what would mama say?"

"Angela, please. I'm not kissing the senorita; Pepe is. You know, daughter, I've kissed my mother, and others on the cheek, but in all my life only one on her lips."

They walked together, Paco, Maria, Michael, Angela, and Fran. The music had started; Pepe and his friends were together, waiting for their turn on the small dance platform.

Though they were dressed for the dance, it was the ladies, and young girls who were the beautiful flowers on that dance platform.

Fran marveled at the dancers, especially Pepe, who stood out, and who was the one the ladies seemed to favor.

"How did he ever learn to dance like that?" Fran said, not really asking a question. There was no real surprise when Angela answered that she and her mother were the ones who taught him. Fran sat somewhat somber until Angela asked him if he was all right. "Yes," he answered." I was just thinking about you and your leaving all this; all this is part of your life."

"Was a part of my life, Francis," she answered. "I've chosen a different life now." She couldn't see his face clearly, and she knew he was still very concerned.

Turning to her father, she said, "Papa, please tell Francis about your dancing."

"You know I couldn't dance at all, daughter. Your mother was the dancer, and she gave up dancing until you were old enough to learn."

She didn't have to see the expression on Fran's face. Just by the strange tautness she felt leave his body, standing close now was enough. He was back on good terms with himself, and their relationship was on firm ground again.

Pepe came to sit with them for a few minutes, saying he needed to rest for a little while. Breathing deeply, he wiped the perspiration off his face with a bandana.

"Having a good time, little brother," Angela asked.

"The best," he answered.

"Do you dance with all the girls?" Fran asked.

"Yes," Pepe said, smiling, "every one, young or old. The best dancers are mostly the older ladies; you watch them, and you'll see."

"One in particular," Paco said, "the widow Garcia, and she's not that old."

"Papa," Angela said, "shame on you."

"I might be old, daughter, but I'm not blind," Paco told her.

"She is one of the best dancers," Pepe said, "and beautiful."

"See, daughter," Paco said.

"I see, Papa," she answered. "Men young can see, and old men can all see very well also."

They were still dancing when Angela, and Fran started back to the adobe.

"Did you think she was beautiful, Francis?"

"Would you want me to say no?" he asked her. "Because if you do, I'd have to lie. You know she is, but not near as beautiful as you are to me, Angela."

They stopped for just a moment to embrace then walked on, Angela smiling in the dark.

Fran was working in the middle of the room when she awoke, separating the things her father had bought. Balancing the packs was important, she knew, plus he was anxious to leave. But she still coaxed him back to bed.

"We have to get our cabin built before winter sets in," he told her.

"I know," she answered. "Just for a minute, please. Then we can get up, and I'll help."

He knew there was no way he could deny her the request.

She did help before going to prepare breakfast, and they did get one pair of pack bags loaded, and balanced. They'd packed mostly the things they wouldn't need on their trip.

Their breakfast was finished before Paco brought the two girls home to meet Francis. Hugging their sister was, of course, their first priority. With his first look, Fran knew what Angela looked like at their age. There was no way a person wouldn't know they were Angela's younger siblings.

They curtsied politely, said they were glad to meet him, and excused themselves, saying they wished to change their clothes. Running off, they were giggling, reminding him of their brother Michael.

"I'm sorry," Angela said.

"About what?" Fran asked.

"They should have stayed a bit longer; it wasn't polite for them to run off like that."

"Let them go; they just got away from being cooped up in school. They'll slow down in a while."

Back at the adobe, Fran balanced out the other saddlebags, and then went to check their horses, making sure there were no problems, such as loose or broken shoes.

Angela went to where the girls were changing, and told them she wasn't happy with the way they ran off. Both said they were sorry, but there were some things they had to do.

"It can wait," she told them. "You have to listen to me first. Both of you sit down."

"Tomorrow Francis and I will finish packing our things, and the day after tomorrow we leave for the mission to be married."

They were excited that their sister was going to be married, but that changed when she said, "Then we will go to the Sierra."

Not realizing exactly what her sister meant, Juana asked, "But when will you return?"

"I don't know," she told them. "Someday for a visit, but not until after we build our house."

"He can't take you away," Barbara said. "I won't let him."

"He's not taking me; I'm leaving with him. He'll be my husband, remember! I was close to becoming an old maid. Would you want that?"

It was time for talk, and tears now for these three sisters, and for the rest of this morning they would stay together. Everything else was forgotten for now.

They ate their midday meal inside this day, with not enough room for everyone at the little table on the veranda. Fran could feel the coolness that emanated from the two young girls. Though he felt sorry for them, it was happening, and they would have to work their way through this. He was hoping they wouldn't begrudge their sister or him their happiness.

After they had eaten, Angela and the girls were helping clear the table, Paco went for his siesta, and Fran walked outside, standing for a minute, just thinking. Angela, coming out, told him, "Go rest for a while; I shouldn't be long," and she gave him a quick kiss. Lying down, he thought more about what had taken place, concerned now about their leaving. One way or another, the day after next he had to leave. Closing his eyes, he slept facing the wall.

Feeling her hand on his shoulder, he smiled with relief; he knew she must have found an answer to the problem. Happily, he asked, "Who's there?" She pulled hard on his shoulder asked, "who, were you expecting?"

Turning to her, he pulled her to him, holding her tightly. Some seconds would pass before she asked, "Are you all right, Francis?"

"I am now," he answered.

"Did you have doubts, Francis?" Angela asked.

"I'm afraid I did," he answered. "After all, they are your family. Tell me how you did it."

"First, I want you to understand there is no one that I would let come between us, no one, ever."

They were even closer now, knowing they had made it over the first rough portion of the trail they'd chosen to ride. To profess their commitment in silence was all they needed, and holding each other, they rested through their siesta.

The water was warming for their bath when Angela told him, "The girls want to see me dance tonight, but I told them I wouldn't, unless you told me it was all right."

"Of course you should dance," he said. "I want to see you dance. But how did you change your sisters about your leaving?"

"It didn't turn out to be that difficult," she told him, "and I told them they were asking me to do something that would be a sacrifice for me. Then I asked if they would return the favor when it came their turn to marry. They realized they were wrong and told me they were sorry. I'm afraid they were selfish in their thinking at first.

"They just didn't realize how much what they wanted was going to affect my life. The solution did turn out to be simple.

"I'm going to get my dress for fiesta, Francis. Watch the water until I get back, please. Then you can wash my back, maybe. All right?"

Coming back in with her dress, she found him standing by the tub holding a washcloth in his hand with a smile on his face. "You're so willing," she said. Putting the dress down, she went to him.

The dress she wore was somewhat more colorful than the brown vaquero clothes he was dressed in. Though they were the correct style, they were rather drab. But who was going to look at him, anyway? Plus he was sure he wasn't going to even try dancing.

Sitting on the edge of the bed, he watched her dress, admiring her beauty, and he wondered how he could have ever thought of riding off alone, but he had.

All dressed, she came over to him, and retied the pale yellow neckerchief he wore. "At first I didn't care for this color you picked, but you look handsome, my love," she told him.

"I guess it isn't the clothes that make the man," he whispered.

Through he didn't feel right without his pistol, Fran left it behind. None of the men here carried arms, and he felt he shouldn't need it.

They ate inside, without Pepe who they knew must be off on some romantic sojoura. Everyone sat rather quietly, and Fran wondered why until the two girls came by his chair. They apologized for what they'd done. "We were not only selfish, but also we behaved poorly," they told him.

"I understand how you feel," Fran said, "and I can only say I am sorry that you have to feel this loss."

He knew this was just one of the things that they would have to work through. Like everyone, there would be other times, and other trails.

The three sisters walked hand in hand while Paco, Maria, and Fran followed close behind. Dancers were already gathering, with Pepe and his friends there, right in the middle. This evening Fran wanted to stay closer to the dance platform, having all his interest in that one particular dancer.

Pepe danced with all three of his sisters, plus many of the other women, and young girls. When Angela danced, he wished he could have been her partner, but he knew you didn't learn to dance the way they danced in a single night.

He first saw the two men out of the corner of his eye as they pushed their way through the crowd. They were taller, and bigger than most of the Mexicans. Only a few feet away, he could see one was being particularly boisterous, and was surely drunk. They were almost to the edge of the dance platform when Fran saw they both had pistols on their hips. The drunkest one had his hands on the edge of the platform when Fran started forward, pushing the people out of his way. The man had just grabbed Juana by the arm when Fran made his leap toward the platform. Juana screamed, and was trying to pull away as Fran took hold of the man by the back of his shirt. Juana's sleeve was torn, but Fran pulled the man away, and as he spun him around he stripped the pistol out of its holster, he pushed the man back away from Juana, and the platform.

The other man stood as the people moved away from around him. Fran, standing at the edge of the platform, the pistol in his hand, said, "Go ahead, if you're so inclined. If not, unbuckle your belt and let it drop."

The man on the ground was trying to stand while reaching for the pistol that wasn't there.

"Where you from?" Fran asked, looking at the man standing.

"We're camped out of town right next to the road."

"Take your friend, and get to your camp. Tomorrow at noon I'll bring you your pistols. Make sure your friend is sober; he has a challenge to meet, and you can be a part of it, if you feel you need too."

The drunk was on his feet now, and had started cussing and talking about how he felt about the greasers and their women.

"Shut your mouth, you damn fool," his partner said, "and let's get out of here. He's no Mexican."

Maria and Angela were both with Juana now. Paco was picking up the pistol and belt. Their fiesta was spoiled this evening as the people disbursed; their evening of celebrating was over. Few would feel like dancing after what had happened.

Fran stuck the pistol in his belt, and was about to move away from the platform when Juana broke away from Maria and Angela and ran to his side. Asking if she could walk with him going home. Angela took his other arm, looked over at her younger sister, and said, "You be careful little sister; Francis belongs to me."

"He saved me from that awful man, Angela. I'm still scared."

At home, Paco gave Fran the pistol belt, and he and Maria took Juana with them. Juana, still visibly shaken by the incident was reluctant to leave, but her father was firm with his request.

Inside, Fran put up the two pistols, and was getting ready for bed. "She's changed her feelings for you, Francis," Angela told him.

"She was frightened," he answered, "that's all, and it will all pass."

"Maybe," Angela said, "but there will always be something there that she'll feel."

"Are you jealous?" he asked.

"Yes," she answered.

"But why? She's only a child."

"No, Francis. Juana is a woman, a young woman, yes, but still a woman, and will probably be married before her next birthday; it's just that way here."

"I'll be happy to be her hero, if she likes," Fran said, "but it's you and I together now, and tomorrow we ride."

"Have you forgotten about noon tomorrow?"

"No," Fran answered. "That shouldn't take all that long."

"But I'm afraid of what might happen."

"Don't be; neither of them is any good with these pistols," he said, and he laid the pistols and belts on the table. "Look, both pistols and belts are new; those are men who don't even know how to wear a gun belt. They might shoot an unarmed man or shoot you in the back, but they're sure not anyone ready to try another man one on one. They're not going to try anything tomorrow, believe me."

He met Paco on the veranda, and had to tell him what he'd told Angela. "We've had their kind here before," Paco said, "but they've never stayed long and never been so brazen."

"There's sure to be more, Paco," Fran told him.

"I don't want Monterey to be like Yerba Buena,"

"Maybe I should talk to some of the other men. You might need them, but I hope not."

Near noon Fran walked out past the veranda, his pistol on, one pistol in his belt, and the pistol belt over his left shoulder. Angela, Maria, and the girls were on the veranda; Paco, and Pepe stepped out with him as he walked toward the road. Halfway there, a dozen men with shovels, and hoes stood waiting. Talking with one of the men, Paco, smiling, turned to Francis and said, "They're gone, and the ashes from their campfires are cold."

Fran, relieved, smiled and said "gracias" to them. "I thank you." Walking back, Fran told Paco, "I think you'll have help if you need it."

CHAPTER X

Thirty minutes later they were ready. "No siesta?" Paco asked. "You ride in the heat of the afternoon."

"No siesta for a few days, for sure, but we don't have a lot of time. We'll get through it, Paco," Fran told him.

They stood by the table on the veranda saying their good-byes. Fran, handing Paco some small leather pouches, said, "Six, one for each of you—you, Maria, and the children. Paco counted the pouches in his hand and knew what the pouches contained.

Fran kissed Maria and then Barbara on both cheeks, but when he bent to kiss Juana she turned her face and met his lips.

They rode away side by side, waving back until the family was out of sight. He looked toward Angela and, though there were tears, she smiled and then said, "See I was right. Did you like that kiss?"

"She's a beautiful young girl, Angela, but she's not you."

They rode off the main road toward the arroyo, where they'd soon feel the heat that radiated from everything there. Even after the sun went down, it remained hot. They stopped near a fairly large pool. Fran watered the horses while she set up their camp. The horses on pickets, the couple played in the water, and then lay on their bed and ate the meal she'd packed before they left.

"I've never eaten this way before," she said.

"How's that?" Fran asked, lying down.?"

"No," she answered, moving closer to him. "You know what I mean. With no clothes on."

They would sleep together that way for most of the night. The heat remained bottled in the narrow arroyo until early morning.

The sun was just turning the tops of the hills bright as they hurriedly dressed, wanting now to exit the arroyo before the sun bearing down would prove to them the arroyo was named correctly. Saddled their horses and rode. She passed him cold tortillas as they rode and, smiling, asked if that was enough to keep his strength up.

"I don't think so, but we'll see, won't we?" he told her, grinning.

They rode out of the arroyo, and into the cooler valley, warm here but not unpleasant. They watered the horses at the river they crossed, and rode on across the flat valley to the Spanish road. There were a few adobes there, where they purchased food, ate, and then rode on. That was the Royal road, she told him, the road between the missions. The padres marked it, and now everyone uses it.

Fran, knowing where the coach road broke off, took it, heading up toward the hills, and the winding grade that would take them over to the mission. "You know this road, Francis?" Angela asked.

"Padre Anthony told me about it when I was at the mission; he said it was the shortest trail to Monterey."

They'd passed over the top, and could see the mission when they stopped to let the horses rest. Angela, dismounting, said, "Let's stay here tonight, Francis."

"But the mission's only a short ride from here," he told her.

"Father Anthony is going to put us in separate rooms, Francis."

"Then let's stay here," Fran answered, dismounting.

The horses watered, Angela led her horse to a grassy knoll and, pointing, told Fran to stay away from those bushes. There he saw it was the same kind of bush that her father had told him about.

The night was warm yet, nothing like the heat they'd endured the previous night camped in the arroyo.

When everything was just right, they could hear music coming from somewhere below.

The night was pleasant; they talked, Fran asking if she was lonesome.

"I miss my family," she said, "but I'm not lonely."

They were dressing in the morning when he saw her put a thong over her head, with a small leather pouch on it.

"I haven't seen that before," he said, "but I've seen Indians that carried medicine pouches that looked similar."

"I guess you could call it my medicine pouch," she answered.

"Colored rocks, dried toad, or lizard tails?" he asked.

She laughed. "No, only one thing there now, the piece of gold you gave my father to give to me.

"And the bag you gave my father before we left, Francis. Six nuggets, not as large as the one you sent to me, but nice. One for each of those we left behind.

"You could have given one to each of us. Why did you give them all to my father?"

"Because the one you already had told him something; so maybe he could find some other answers. It's only because of that one you carry that I now have you, so if it happened to me, why not something for them?"

"You are a romantic, Francis. My father is too, but I love you both for it."

Father Anthony welcomed them, and hearing they wished to marry, said, "he'd marry them that very day." They ate with the padre, and were married with two of the local mission workers in attendance. When the padre asked for the ring, Fran took it out of the pouch he carried.

They watched as their names were entered into the record book. Then the padre looked back in the records for Angela, and found the names of her mother and father, there from twenty years before.

They were shown their room there by the mission, and afterwards walked to watch the dancers. That night they'd hear the guitars, and the ballads sung by some lonely lover.

He'd told Padre Anthony they must leave early the next morning. "We have to build a cabin before winter," Fran said. The Padre said he under stood, and he'd see them in the morning.

Their horses were already saddled, and tied by their door when they went out in the morning. A quick breakfast, and they'd load their things before the padre came to give them his blessing.

"The road across the pass is dangerous, my son," the padre said. "I'm afraid you may find some men of dubious character plying that very same route. Be cautious."

"We will, Father," Fran told him, and gave the padre the small leather pouch he'd fixed for him. Early risers from the mission came to see them off, bidding them "via con Dios" with the padre. Leaving, they rode side by side, each leading a packhorse.

They hadn't traveled but a short way when Angela asked, "The ring. How did you know my size?"

"I didn't," Fran told her, "but Maria did."

"She didn't tell me," Angela said.

"Was she supposed to?" Fran asked.

"I guess not, but she could have," she said. "But I'm glad she didn't."

On reaching the wagon trail, they fell in behind a wagon, and moved along in the dust and then the heat. The trail followed the bottom of a canyon, a sluggish stream with green, slimy water in pools here and there.

Coming to the grade up into the pass, they moved slower as some heavy wagon ahead slowed to a crawl. Then, nearly to the top, the line came to a complete halt. There was a natural winter drainage draw alongside the road here, and a cattle trail that they could easily negotiate with their horses. "Follow me," Fran said, riding down into the draw, then up onto the cattle trail.

It was an easy trail for them, but it would be impossible for a wagon. They'd passed half a dozen wagons, all stopped on the wagon trail. Moving ahead, they heard a man holler, "Hey, you damn Mex, get back in line." Pulling to the side, he motioned Angela to pass, then rode in behind her. He looked back, and saw him walking up alongside the wagons but continued on. Almost to the top, a heavily loaded wagon with a broken wheel had the road blocked.

Two men with a long, heavy pole, and a block were trying to pry the axel up so another man could work on the hub. There was not quite enough weight to make the pry, so Fran dismounted, and told Angela to hold the horses. He hung his belt on the saddle horn and running over, put his weight on the pole with the two men.

The wagon raised, an older man removed the hub of the broken wheel. He had a bit of a struggle but got the new wheel on, and the washer and nut. They'd just let the wagon down, and were moving it out of the way, so the other wagons could pass, when the man reached them.

He was all red-faced and sweaty, a rather large, foul-mouthed man cussing, and ranting about damned greasers passing everyone on the trail.

The older man stepped out in front of the man and said, "Leave the kid alone. He came and helped." He would have none of it and, was telling the old man he'd slap his mouth closed if he didn't shut up.

Fran by then had his belt buckled on, holster tied down, and was lifting the thong off the hammer of his pistol as he walked toward the two men. Stopping, he said, "Let him be, Pop. I'm the one he wants." The older man turned, and stepped quickly aside, almost as surprised as the man with the big mouth.

He had a pistol on his hip, and, like most, it was too high and not tied down, plus there was a thong over the hammer. Fran just stood; he wanted the man to get a good look and realize just how bad a position he was in. He wouldn't be able to lift the thong, let alone clear his holster in time.

"Use it," Fran said, "or unbuckle it and let it drop. You can pick it up when you bring up your wagon."

"I ..." was all that came out of his mouth, and he dropped the belt, turned, and walked back the way he came.

Picking up the pistol, Fran removed the caps, and then shoved the barrel of the pistol down into the soft dirt by the side of the trail. Putting it back into the holster, he looped the thong over the hammer, and dropped it by the side of the wagon trail.

The old man stood smiling. Fran said, "See you, Pop." He was walking toward Angela, and his horse when he heard the old man say, "My thanks to you, young fella."

Reaching Angela he put his arms around her, holding her. "You all right?" Francis asked.

"I'm all right now," she answered, "but what's wrong with men like that?"

"I don't know," he answered, "but there's going to be more like him."

"He called you a Mexican, Francis, and you're not."

"But I'm dressed like one, and I guess that's all he saw or cared to see."

The wagon trail here on top was wide, and they could easily ride past those slower-moving wagons, which would soon come to the downward slope, and a narrower road. Fran looked off toward the north along the top of the higher ground. There were game, and cattle trails that followed the higher ground then sloped off to the east and down toward the valley below.

When he rode away from the wagon trail, Angela asked why he was leaving it. "We don't need any more trouble," he answered. She was happy to be away from the men, some she felt, who were, mean, arrogant, dirty bullies, that she even feared. But she wondered now where they were heading.

"Do you know this trail, Francis?"

He had to smile. "I don't know that one, and I don't know this way either, but we'll find our way."

She didn't mind it being just the two of them; they had everything they needed, and they had enough to feed themselves for weeks, actually.

They followed a trail that dropped gradually down into the broad valley they could now see. Their general direction of travel was east, and slightly north. The direction Francis knew would take them to the Sierra and Charley.

It was long past their noon stop, and was really too early to make their night camp, but a stream and good grass was important. Finding it just then would keep them here for the rest of the day and night. The horses all taken care of and the wood gathered, Fran sat with his back against one of the packs, gazing out over the valley they had to cross. It was a large, flat expanse, hot, almost desert like. But he could see the reflected light from water, and trees in meandering lines that meant water. They were areas that could be wet, or maybe just winter streams that might be dry this time of year. But green areas too that he felt could be meadow. He dug his telescope out of his saddlebag, and continued looking. Maybe there was a road that they could travel east on. There was no visible route, but there were some places where the brush looked sparse, and he saw lines that might be part of a trail. She asked if he saw a way. "No," he answered, "but there has to be a way, and we'll find it."

The telescope back into his saddlebag, he took out the pistols he picked up in Monterey. Pulling all the lead, he dumped the powder, cleaned each pistol thoroughly, and packed them away. Taking out the pistol he'd worn before, he buckled it on. "Going to wear two pistols, Francis?" Angela asked.

"I will," he answered, "but for now it can hang on my saddle horn." "They're sure to draw some attention, and I'll hear someone say pistolero, but they'll also command a certain amount of respect that were not getting now." He took her pistol, and buckled it securely to her saddle horn. "You don't have to wear it," he told her, "but you'll have it close, just in case you need it." He knew she wasn't fond of firearms, but would tolerate the pistol there. Because she did realize it was a necessary precaution, and for protection.

The stream was small, but they could stand in a shallow pool and with one of their cooking pots pour water over themselves. Lying together after dark they looked up into a clear sky full of stars, listened to the coyote calls, and watched for shooting stars.

The first rays were just showing over the far-off Sierras as Fran saddled the horses. Then they were riding down the slope when the sun's full brightness faced them.

At the bottom of the slope they crossed a seldom-used wagon trail. The road went north, but Fran knew they needed to go east. They followed the road, coming to a trail that would take them east, and wide enough for their packhorse. The brush was tall here, and Fran could only see the sky, but it didn't make much difference; there were no landmarks that he would be able to use anyway.

As the sun moved up so did the temperature, and Fran remembered the desert on the other side of the Sierra. The dust and debris from the high brush, along with the heat, made it difficult to breathe, and they were glad when they broke out onto lower-growing brush.

There were patches of white ground here, some quite large, and Fran remembered that it was alkali. And could be dangerous if the ground under them was wet. These could be a death trap for unsuspecting large animals.

Large rabbits bounded away from the bunch grass areas they rode through, and Fran thought maybe a couple for supper. But he remembered that the smaller rabbits, which he saw a few of, here were much better eating. The trail they followed now meandered along a line of trees and, shallow grassy, dry depressions. There was grass for the horses, but water was what they really needed.

They came upon a small pool first, which had enough water, but was warm. They let the horses drink then pushed on following that same depression, hoping to find more, and better water. They kept moving, and gradually the pool sizes increased until they came onto large pools, ample grass for their mounts, and wood for a fire. It was an early camp again, but they hadn't given the horses a noon rest, and didn't know what they could expect to find ahead.

The last thing they did was gather firewood, and then Angela went with him to hunt for their supper. The heat of the day was still high, so the rabbits were scarce. Fran succeeded in bagging only one. "It's too hot to eat anyway," she told him. "That's enough for us this evening."

She made some tortillas, as he watched the rabbit cooking and enjoyed his coffee, with brown Mexican sugar. The water was too tepid to be palatable, but it was all right for coffee.

After eating, they bathed in the pool, then, lay on top of their bed without drying off.

"Not much of a honeymoon," he said.

"I don't see how it could be any better," she answered. "Except for an apple, it's the Garden of Eden."

"Then maybe a couple of fig leaves."

"No," he added, "from the way a fig leaf feels against my hands, no."

They stayed most of the night on top of their bedroll, but when they let their fire burn down, the mosquitoes forced them under the covers.

Dressing as fast as they could in the morning, they built the fire up, laughing together at their plight.

"They've spoiled our Garden of Eden," Angela said.

"An invasion of pests," he said seriously.

"Oh, it's not all that bad," she told him.

"It's a lot worse," he answered. "Not the mosquitoes, Angela. I was thinking about the men coming here to this land. We'd better ride, I want to get to where Charley is."

He left the fire to go gather their horses. Minutes later they were again moving east. There were streams to cross, but they were low this time of the year, and he followed the trails to where the wild animals crossed. Always testing the crossing before leading the heavily laden packhorses across.

The foothills, and the Sierra could plainly be seen now. Here as the ground started to rise, they'd leave the reedy ponds, the alkali and marshy flats, and hopefully, the pesky mosquitoes behind. Then on to a wagon trail that followed along the lower edge of the foothills. Other travelers they'd find here, and the second belt he'd hung over his saddle horn he buckled on. Onto the road that headed north they went, through rolling, grass-covered hills and oak trees.

With no idea how far they were from the stream he'd worked in, he could only hope he'd recognize it, or the country near there. He knew, though, if he did miss it, he wouldn't turn back until they reached the wagon trail, he and the others had followed over the Sierra.

Just a few wagons and riders were on the road, but the men looked the same, and he wondered how he could tell if any one of these men was good or bad.

Every watercourse they crossed had been camped by, many times. Now, the areas fouled by those very people who had stopped there before. He moved off onto a game trail away from the wagon trail to look for a secluded spot with water, where they could spend the night. It was another early camp, but he knew they were getting close; he didn't need to hurry now.

The horses taken care of, they'd gathered their firewood and were sitting by the fire when she asked if he was all right. "I'm fine," Fran answered. "Why?"

"You've been awfully quiet," Angela said. "Aren't you glad you'll be home soon?"

"What home, Angela? There is no home; I'm bringing you to where there's nothing, just a piece of land."

"It's all right, Francis. We'll build our cabin; I can help," she said. "You'll see; everything will be fine."

They lay on their bedroll watching the fire, listening to the night sounds, and their horses cropping grass.

Riding down off the higher ground and onto the road, where they could again ride side by side, most of the time.

They drew long looks from many of the other travelers, dressed like vaqueros, though in subdued colors. Angela, with her hair up under her sombrero, should pass as a juvenile, but an armed juvenile. But it was Fran who would draw the somewhat untrusting but respectful long looks, with his double sidearm, and his somewhat somber look.

He moved off the wagon trail again, heading up to higher ground before picking a place for their night camp. At their campfire, Fran apologized for his continued dour feeling, adding, "but the way these people look at us is getting to me."

"Your pistols could be a part of what's drawing those looks, Francis," she told him.

"I'm sure that's a part of it," he answered, "but they're probably the only thing that keeps the scum at bay."

"Aren't you being a bit harsh, Francis?"

"Believe me, Angela, I'm not; you've only seen a part of what's already here, and I'm afraid there's going to be a lot more of the same kind coming here."

Chapter XI

In the morning they dropped from the higher ground, and he felt they had to be getting close. He didn't say anything to Angela, because he wasn't quite sure.

The morning was half gone when they came around the low hill that jutted out into the valley, just a little farther than most. The expanse of grass ahead looked familiar, but the posts placed ever few hundred feet were not. Out in the open where he could look east, he saw the cache he had helped to build. But here again, something was different—a small building close to the base of the cache. When he saw the stream, he was positive; he knew he was back.

Coming to the trail that led toward the cache he smiled at Angela and said, "This is it; we've made it." They rode toward it, and the small building, and then he saw the three figures. One tall but two smaller ones that scurried off as they drew near, Fran knew Charley from just the way he stood. He'd seen Charley so many times before he'd recognize him anywhere.

Charley stood silent right up to the time Fran dismounted; then they put their arms around each other, and began slapping the dust from each other's back. "Good to see you, old man," Fran said. But Charley was looking at the other rider, who was still in the saddle. She took off her sombrero, and shook out her hair. "Well," Charley said, "my goodness, what have we got here?" Fran, stepping away from him, said, "Charley, my wife Angela."

"An angel she is, Francis," Charley said, causing Angela to blush.

After helping her down, Charley helped Fran unloaded the horses next to the cache. There they'd store what food that was left from their trip.

Angela asked Charley if she could use the fire that burned near his little cabin. "I'd like to cook a decent meal," she said, "something a little better than what we've been having on the trail."

"Could you cook enough for a few others?" Charley asked.

"How many?" she asked,

"Eight," Charley answered.

Angela looked toward Fran said, "but I don't have a pot large enough."

"I have a big pot," Charley told her, "but fill it up and yours too, so there'll be plenty."

"Who, Charley?" Fran asked. Charley pointed to the southeast, to the shallow draw that led into the hills. Fran could see what appeared to be two large piles of brush and a, tiny bit of smoke curling up out of the top of one of them, and barely visible.

"There are two Indian families," Charley said. "They asked if they could camp there. Couldn't turn them down; it's not safe for them out there. Seems some out there feel they're fair game, and shoot them for sport.

"Then there's a young woman, and her son. You might have seen them run off when you came up. They're what's left of a family that got shot up a while back."

Angela asked if she could have the other pot, and added wood to the fire. The pot there, she put water in it, Charley put it on to heat, as went on talking.

"The other families found them when they went out foraging, and brought them here," he said. "The boy had a large splinter in his foot, which was infected, and he was fevered some. His mother had starved and was down to no more then skin and bones. How long they'd been hiding out there I don't know, but they were in bad shape. I bathed the boy's foot, got the splinter out, and then kept him soaking that foot to keep the poison coming.

"We heated water, and the other two women, fed them and with clean clothes on put them down to bed in a corner of my little cabin. They've been there for some weeks now, and doing well but their scared of everyone except me, and the other Indians."

The boy was peeking around the cabin, and Angela called "muchacho" and waved for the boy to come. Slowly the boy moved toward them; reluctantly he came, but he stayed next to Charley. He limped just a little, had moccasins on his feet, and wore an altered man's shirt with no sleeves.

"One of my old shirts," Charley said, "but he doesn't seem to mind."

Angela made a cup of chocolate, and gave it to Charley, and told him, "You give it to him; he trusts you."

"He came out when you called, Angela," Charley said.

"A female voice," she said, "and he could be a little more familiar with Spanish."

"Hmm," Charley mused, "never thought about that, but I don't know that many words in Spanish anyway"

Handing the cup to the boy he said, "Here yaw go, Rabbit, Angela made you something nice."

One small sip, and the boy smiled, took the cup with him, and walked to the cabin, disappearing around the corner.

"He'll go share with his mother," Charley said. "They're real close that way."

Angela was soon rewarded for the chocolate she made, when the woman came to the fire with her son.

"There are more cups of chocolate," Angela said," but the beans would take a while." She started making tortillas that she was certain they'd be familiar with, and would readily eat.

They were both staying close to Charley, reluctant to move very far away from his side. "You might have inherited yourself a family," Fran told him.

"She's a might young for an old coot like me," Charley said.

"She and the boy need you, Charley," Angela told him. "If you don't feel too uncomfortable about it, just let her make the decision."

"Guess I'd better think about a bigger cabin," Charley answered. Angela and Fran were now both smiling.

Fran was up in the cache, and Charley tied on the sacks of beans, flour, and corn meal for Fran to pull up, and store. They'd store all the food except for what they'd need for a day or two. That done, Fran said, "I guess I'd better bag a deer; with this many to feed we're going to need it."

"There's a fella comes by with a wagon, said if I ever need anything to just say the word," Charley said. "Sez he's gonna haul freight for the miners. I had to laugh when he told me it was easier for him to mine the miners then dig for gold his self."

"Sounds smart to me," Fran said. "It's no fun working in that cold water."

"Would you work at it if you didn't have to work in the water?" Charley asked. "Probably," Fran answered, "but I don't like digging underground like a mole, either. Why?"

"I'll show you one day after the cabins are up."

The beans were still cooking as they talked about how big the cabins should be. Charley said, if they built them together they could save logs, and labor by having the wall in the center a common wall between them. That was fine with Fran, but he wondered why Charley didn't want to build the cabins right where they were.

"Look from here to the two fence posts that are the closest together," Charley said, "then from there, to the stream. You can see that would be a more natural curve for the stream than the route it takes now. Then behind us is the spring where we get our water right?"

"That's right," Fran answered, "but I still don't understand."

"All right," Charley went on, "if you walk east over the hill behind us where will you end up?"

"At the curve in the stream," Fran said.

"Then if that hill wasn't there, then the stream would run right through here where we're sitting."

"But the hill is there, Charley," Fran said.

"But at one time it wasn't; that hill is an old landslide. You go up to the mountainside above it, and you can see where it all came from, some long time past."

Fran sat thinking for a minute then said, "Then we're sitting right over where the old stream used to be."

"I hit it when I dug down inside the cabin there, and it's only a foot and a half to two foot down to gravel, and then a foot or so to bedrock."

"Good color, Charley?" Fran asked.

"Much better than the new streambed where we worked in the water."

"Now what, Charley?" Fran asked.

"It's in the bank," Charley said. "We can work some of it sometime if we need it; right now we'll use it for our road down from here to the wagon road, all right?"

"That sounds good," Fran answered. "Right now we need shelter; winter's just around the corner."

"Well, I'm sure there ain't no king's ransom, Francis, but you could buy a hell of a lot of beans with what's under there."

Charley sent Rabbit to get the other families when Angela said, "The beans are ready."

She sat right next to Charley, and seemed a bit relaxed now. "Never did know her name," Charley said, smiling at the Indian woman, "but she reminded me of a dove the way they put themselves in harm's way to save their young, so I call her Dove, and she doesn't seem to mind."

Angela worried about having enough utensils to serve everyone, but she worried for naught. The little families brought their own wooden bowls, spoons, and reed mats to sit on. No cups, but there were enough tin cups of theirs to give the three children chocolate. Dove went to the cabin, and brought back tin ware for Charlie, Rabbit, and herself.

Speaking Spanish, Angela saw that the adults did understand a smattering of the language. They knew that the padres or the Mexicans from the ranchos on the other side of the valley did have some influence on these people.

The pots were empty, and Angela said, "I hope everyone had enough."

"There was plenty," Charley said. "We've eaten more this day than we've eaten in a long while. Dove gets a few meals like that then maybe she'll put on a pound or two.

Angela started picking up their things, and Dove was there to help. The little families picked up their things, and the adults all said, "Gracias."

Angela answered, "You're welcome," in Spanish, "No hay de que."

Charley sat by the fire, and told Angela, "When that freighter comes by I'll let him know what we need. He'll bring it when he returns; you tell me what you need, and I'll see to it."

The horses taken care of Fran, fixed their night camp under the cache. With the canvas from their packsaddle, they would have a bit of privacy. With a couple of pots of warm water they could bathe and, then relax for a while before dark. Fran said, "he'd like to get an early start. Be nice to have some fresh meat for a couple of meals."

Out of bed early, Fran had the fire burning bright when Charley walked up. "Might just as well start on the logs we're going to need," he told Fran.

"If I get back early," Fran said, "I'll come up, and give you a hand."

"I'll stay working close by until you get back, Francis. You stay around camp; it's just not safe with no one here to protect what we have. That's why I couldn't get a lot done before. I had to work within eyesight," Charley said. "I'll have Pito and Pino give me a hand. We can make a few stakes, and at least stake out the cabin site."

Fran brought his horse, and saddle up as Angela made him a quick breakfast. He rode off not long after the sun was up, wanting to get something and get back as quickly as possible. He knew there was a lot of work to be done.

Less than an hour out, and he saw the first deer, a doe. But he waited, knowing there had to be other deer close by. Only a couple of minutes later, he saw the buck. It was not a real big buck, but it would do. Two minutes later he was leading his horse up into the patch of brush where he'd shot the animal. He field dressed it, covered his saddle with a tarp, a couple of ties, and he was leading the horse home.

He passed Charley, and his two helpers with a couple of trees down.

"Clean them up, Charley," he hollered. "I'll drag them down after I take care of this buck."

Back in camp he dropped the deer off, and all three Indian girls were there, and went to work. All Fran had to do was wash his tarp in the stream, pick up the ropes he needed, and ride back up to where Charley had felled the trees. With the single horse he could only drag one log at a time. But before lunch was ready he had both logs down at the cabin site.

Now he could start peeling the bark, and they'd have the first two house logs. Near noon, and a good half a day's work done, he went to the stream to wash.

Walking back, he was savoring the aroma of liver and onions frying, as Charley and his two helpers were walking in.

"Smell the cooking, Charley?" Fran asked.

"Couldn't help it," Charley answered, "that smell could drive a hungry man mad, and right now I could chew up the frying pan."

There was not enough liver to satisfy everyone's hungry, but the venison steaks took care of the rest of their needs. Satisfied, and with the sun high, they'd take a rest, and finish their day's labor later in the day.

That work went on day after day. Fran brought in a couple more deer, but said he'd have to go farther out now, having taken enough of the locals. There were a couple of big, old, mossy horn bucks, but they'd be tough, and their horns would make poor soup.

The base logs set, they started stacking on the wall logs. The girls dried the meat they didn't consume in a day or two; then stored that in the cache for later.

Charley made a sign for the freighter asking him to stop. Then Angela told him the two girls; Cana and Alta, should go gather acorns.

"Gonna slow us up a bit," Charley said, "but they know what's needed to survive in this country. I'll stay in camp, Francis, if you'll take a couple of packhorses, go keep them company, and out of trouble. Don't need them shot up like Dove's family. You can move around a bit and keep the varmints away better than me."

Angela got the others together, and gathered the things they'd need the next morning. A lunch had to be packed, and a lunch left for Charley, because Dove told Angela she would go and help. They left early the next morning; Pino and Pito leading the way, north and slightly east to where the oak trees were thick, and the acorns plentiful.

Aleta, Cana, and Dove stopped for a few minutes to collect or dig something out of the ground, putting everything in the baskets and bags they carried. At the low hills, and flats where the oak trees were, they stopped. Fran put the horses on pickets, and moved to a spot where he could cover the area well. Even the little ones picked up the acorns that were so plentiful under every tree. He'd been watching for close to two hours when he heard the warblelike whistle that he attributed to an owl. Owls he should only hear in the late evenings, and this was very close to midday. Looking out over those picking up the acorns, he saw that Pico was missing.

He was at a quandary now; he didn't know what that call might mean, but he was fairly sure it wasn't an owl.

He checked everyone working, all there but Pico. Then he heard the horses on the trail that led right to where they were gathering acorns. Horses for sure, and that meant riders. He'd have to beat them to the rise above, where they could easily see those gathering acorns, Angela one of them.

He was trotting through the oaks, not wanting to be out of breath. He stopped behind a large oak next to the trail. The riders wouldn't see him until he stepped out, blocking the trail.

He was thinking about the sound the owl made, and what Angela told him when he met Pito. His name meant, "whistle" in Spanish. Then it was Pito who warned him, not an owl. Now he hoped that Pito was close by.

As he stepped out onto the trail, he knew these two sitting up on horses could easily see Angela and the others gathering acorns. "That's about far enough," he said, and both men pulled up their mounts. Well, the lead rider snorted, "What have we got here?" The second rider, moving his horse alongside, said, "You're dressed like a Mex, but you don't talk like one."

"True enough," Fran answered.

"Looks like you've got a few hens in your flock, my friend," he said to Fran, smiling. "Maybe you could use a couple of roosters in your henhouse."

"I thought I might be able to handle this with everyone on good terms," Fran said, "but I'd say you two are not the most honorable type."

"What the hell do you think you're going to do," the rider asked. There's two of us; you might get one of us, but the other one's going to get you."

Fran, tense, now knew these two were not going to capitulate; they were ready, and the odds were in their favor."

Fran whistled and hoped for the best. When he heard the answer, he knew the doubt he had felt, now fell on those two riders' shoulders.

"One of you will take one from the front; the other one is going to get it in the back. I tried to be halfway decent with you," he said, a little commanding authority in his voice, "but vermin like you don't deserve respect. Now unbuckle your gun belts, and let them drop."

"You can't do this," one of them told him.

"Tell me why?" Fran asked. "But while you talk, drop them or your maggot fare." Both belts dropped to the ground. "Now, with your left hand, your long guns, slow and easy." The rifles dropped. "You're free to go, but if I see you again, they'll be no small talk."

Fran watched as they rode away, making sure they went out through the trees below, and out into the more open country. He was fairly sure they wouldn't try to double back without their weapons.

He saw Pito moving over with the others, and waited there until he felt it was time to pack up and head for camp.

He was surprised at the bags of acorns they had picked, but he balanced the packs as best he could, and loaded the horses. Ready to start back, he picked up the weapons, and hung them on the packsaddles. Turning to pick up the lead lines, he saw Angela looking at the guns, with a puzzled frown on her face. She didn't ask about them then, but he knew he'd have some explaining to do before he'd get any sleep this night.

He unloaded the horses, then while he took care of them; Angela was busy making tortilla. The venison they had dried and rubbed with chili, she heated in a frying pan, then wrapped in a warm tortillas. This, for the most part, was their supper this evening. Some bulbs, previously dug up were peeled, and divided between everyone. They had a sweet, nutty flavor they enjoyed, and a few more would have been even better. Now Fran thought about going out gathering, how it was always going to be a danger, especially for the women but also for Pito, Pino, and the little ones.

He had just sat down, and Charley saw his chance to find out about the arms he'd brought in. He asked when he was going to hear the story. "I'd like to hear it too," Angela told him.

Fran told them what had happened, and how Whistle had warned him with what he first thought was a bird. Telling the story Whistle heard his name spoken, and saw Charley, Angela, and Fran look toward him. He smiled, knowing Fran was explaining what had happened.

"I should show Whistle, and Pino how to use the guns," Fran said. "Then they'd have something to fight back with."

"No,' Charley told him, "they'd be blamed for every white man shot anyplace around here, then hunted down, and killed like some dog."

"No, we'll just have to keep them under our wing for a while. Puts a bit of a load on us, I know, but they've been pulling their weight, and we'll just have to keep a vigil, Francis."

"While you were up picking acorns that freighter came by. I gave him the list; be a couple weeks, though. But there's nothing there we can't do without for a while."

"Tomorrow could one of you help me bring in a couple of large rocks?" Angela asked. "We need them to work the acorns into meal. They can't go to where they usually do that work unless they could camp there for a few days."

'Well do it," Charley said, "but one of the girls will have to pick out the rocks."

In the morning they decided, Dove would go with Charley. It wasn't too far; they could easily walk up, and back before noon. Rabbit was happy to stay with Angela, have chocolate, and learn how to speak both Spanish and English. "He's smart," Angela said, "and it is easier for children to learn; they can just pick it up, just being around people talking."

Fran and Angela watched as Charley, and Dove started off toward the slope, walking, and holding hands.

Fran, Whistle, and Pino would work on the cabin, peeling and cutting the notches in the ends of the logs. The walls were going up, and once the walls were done the work would be easier. The ridgepole, rafters and roof beams, made of much lighter logs, would be a lot easier to work with. After that it was shingle the roof, and they'd have their winter shelter.

When Charley and Dove came walking down, she was smiling, but Charley was shaking his head. "The rocks she wants ain't rocks; they're boulders. They must weigh close to four hundred pounds. We'd wear out every piece of chain and rope we have trying to drag them down." He sat down, and thought for a few minutes, and then told Fran it's either a sled or a travois.

"I think a sled would work; it's all down hill and at a slight slope, But it's going to take all of us just to get them on aboard. Shouldn't take us more than a day to get them down. That's after we build the sled.

"Something else though, I did find a good clay bank where we can get the clay we'll need to chink the logs; gonna need some tree moss too. That will take most of another day plus a lot of walking."

CHAPTER XII

Charley spent the rest of the afternoon gathering the limbs and other material he needed, and then he worked on the sled. He worked quietly, and even when they ate he seemed to be mulling something over in his mind. Really out of character for Charley, Fran knew, but he'd wait for him to make the first move. If he needed help he'd ask for it.

As usual everyone retired early after all the work they'd done every day, and tomorrow would be much of the same. Fran did tell Angela he felt Charley was troubled. "Dove seems happier now," Angela told him. "I don't think there's a problem there, and she looks so much better since she's gained a little weight.

Fran or Angela was usually the first to get up and start the morning fire, but this morning the fire was burning brightly, and Fran could smell the coffee before he was on his feet. At the fire they found Charley already sipping on a hot cup. Fran poured a cup, and sat down. "You're up earlier than usual. You all right, Charley?"

"I'm fine; just got a bit of a problem."

"Can I help?" Fran asked.

"I don't really know," Charley answered. "It's Dove."

Fran and Angela looked at each other, neither having any idea what could be wrong.

"She's been staying with Rabbit until he falls to sleep, and then she's been coming into my bed."

Fran wanted to smile, but he kept a straight face and asked, "Is that wrong, Charley? She needs you."

"I'm old enough to be her father," Charley said.

"If she wants things that way Charley, are you going to turn her away? She's depending on you and needs you, Charley," Angela said. "Don't hurt her by rejecting her."

"I need her too," Charley said. "Her and Rabbit mean a lot to me."

"That should be it then, Charley. You both have something you need," Fran said, pouring Charley more coffee, then told him "Let's get ready for winter."

"Charley, could you bring some clay for me?" Angela asked.

"Sure, but what for?"

"I'd like to build a horno," she answered, "an oven, so we could bake bread."

I'll bring the clay, and you show me what you want, and I'll build it. I do like bread."

With the rocks down, and set in place they started removing the hulls from the acorns. But the rocks were outside, exposed to the inclement weather. They now needed to build a roof over them, and Charley said, "we might just as well build it large enough to protect the oven, he and Angela were going to build."

With the clay, and the moss they had picked from the oak trees, they chinked the house logs, working the clay and the moss and, wearing the skin raw on their hands.

With much of that work done, the women were at the rocks grinding the acorns into meal, and then leaching out the tannin. Now, not only sore fingers, brown dyed sore fingers. But they worked on content, knowing they would soon have something to add to their food supply. Then next steps would be much easier—the meal rinsed thoroughly with hot water, the tannin gone, and the meal spread to dry. The dried meal added to breads, or cookies gave them a nutty flavor, but it could also be eaten as gruel, or mixed in the batter for their griddlecakes.

Angela and Fran moved into the cabin, anxious to get their things under a roof, concerned about it raining. Dove and Charley continuing with the work on their side of the cabin. The table they'd been using outside, they put on the veranda, under cover, with the chairs and a bench. They could handle about any winter weather now.

Their fire now close to the cabin, Charley and Fran were talking about where they would start fencing. It was then that Fran told Charley about being concerned that the deer were becoming scarce. "The miners must be paying well for meat, because the men hunting are killing everything.

"I'll take Whistle with me, and we'll try down in the tulles for elk, but I'll bet they're hunting there too."

They saw the wagon turn off the road, and moving toward them. "Must be Bart," Charley said. "He should be bringing the things I ordered."

"I'll go give him a hand," Fran said, and, walked out to meet the freighter.

After parking the freighter's wagon they took the horses to the river to drink, then put them out on pickets. Fran brought the freighter to the table and Charley introduced him.

"There enough for another mouth?" Charley asked Angela. Waving the spoon she had in her hand, she answered, "Plenty."

"I hate to impose on people," Bart said, "but I got a problem, there's been four riders shadowing me for a ways." I had to sneak out of camp in the middle of the night when I saw them setting up near me. I'd be beholden to you, Charley, if you'd let me stay here a day or two. They could be waiting for me to collect for this load, and then knock me over. I've got a scattergun, but I couldn't better four of them."

"You stay." Charley told him. "Maybe we can figure something out."

After eating, Bart thanked Angela, and the other women. Telling them, "it was a fine meal." "I'll sleep under my wagon tonight," he said. "See you in the morning."

"What do you think?" Charley asked.

"Can't blame him, Charley," Fran answered. "I'd be concerned too if I was him. Got any ideas?"

"Let me sleep on that one," Charley told him.

It was the first night in the new cabin, and they'd have to sleep on the dirt floor, but there was the straw they brought in. They needed a bed, but a table, and chairs were important too, maybe not as much so, but still needed.

They unloaded the freight wagon right where it stood. Then put most of the food up into the cache. The two stoves, and windows they carried over to the cabins. It was more work but easy work, and under a roof.

Four riders did ride by going north. "That's them I'm sure," Bart said. "I wonder if they're heading back."

"The way they were looking us over, I doubt it," Charley told him.

Bart helped them with the stoves, and connecting the pipes. They had the stoves in, but they really didn't need heat inside yet.

The riders didn't show themselves again, but they figured they could still be around, so Fran dug out his telescope. The most logical spot for someone to watch from was the high ground to the north, and on the other side of their little valley. Sitting in the shade on the veranda, he scanned that ridge for thirty minutes before the lookout moved, and gave himself away. "Probably figured no one would see him unless he stood out in the open. You'd be impossible to see, mister, if I didn't have this telescope," Fran said, to himself.

Going to where Bart and Charley were, he found Charley was just paying Bart. It was not a really large amount of gold but enough, and he figured he would be probably be, easy pickings for those four men. Plus Bart just might have something more he'd collected with him.

Fran told them he'd seen the lookout, and from where he was watching there was no way they could make a move, at least not during the day. They moved to the table on the veranda, and over coffee tried to figure what Bart could do to escape. But alone there really was no way he could leave. There was no law, they knew, and they were all there was. Yet by helping him they knew, they were putting themselves in jeopardy too.

Everyone was there now as they talked. Fran said, that he might be able to hide in the back of Bart's wagon and surprise them if they did attack. "Damn poor odds," Charley said, "two against four, and if they got wise they might just hit us here, and raise havoc. No, better we just wait, but be ready."

Bart told them there'd been a couple of miners shot at their claims, plus other people on the roads. "I'm beginning to think these four might be the fellows responsible for some of it," he said.

"Sure could be," Charley said, "but there's not much we can do other than keep a sharp eye, and sit."

"I think I'll go find where they're camped," Fran told them. "I go," he heard Whistle answer, and looking toward Fran, pointed to himself and then to Fran. "You and I?" Fran asked, and Whistle nodded. "Guess he's picking up the English language a bit," Charley said.

"That ain't even really two words, "Fran answered."

"He never says any more than he has to," Charley said, "not even in sign language, but he'll sure let you know what he wants."

"I'm not going to go tonight," Fran said. "I want to see if they keep that lookout up there, and I have to get some things ready."

Wagons and riders both moved north and south on the road with apparently no problems. But of course if they weren't traders or freighters, they wouldn't likely be carrying enough for those fellas to bother with.

Before Fran retired, he took out his buckskins pants and shirt, well worn but soft and quiet when he walked, and then a pair of moccasins.

"I don't like it, Francis," Angela said. "I'm scared; there's something that's just not right.

"I know, and that's why I have to look. I'm not going to try anything, honest. Just check."

"You promise?" she asked.

"I promise," he answered.

After breakfast Fran again looked toward that high ground and the area where the lookout had been sitting. 'You're late." he said under his breath, when the man did show. He sat down back in the shade, and Fran wondered if the man was using a telescope. From this distance he wouldn't be able to tell unless he caught that telltale flash off the glass. That wouldn't happen if he remained back there in the shade.

Whistle and Pino stood by the table watching Fran. He took the telescope and, handing it to Whistle, pointed to the hill where the lookout sat. This telescope was something strange, to Whistle, and it took him awhile, to find what he was looking for. He sat down to rest an elbow on the table, and then smiled with satisfaction. When he started to hand the glass back, Fran pointed to Pino, saying, "Let Pino take a look."

Leaving, Fran went inside. He just had to get the bed frame made. He worked awhile then went out to check on the lookout. Whistle and Pino were now helping with the acorns. The bed was put together, plus pegs in the log walls where they could hang their coats and Fran's rifle near the door.

At their late supper, the lookout was still there at his spot on the shoulder of the hill. Everyone sat on the veranda with them watching and waiting until the look out got up and left. The next day they went about their work as usual, except Bart. He stayed most of the time watching, and asking Fran about the lookout on the hill.

After they'd eaten Fran went inside, when he came back out he was dressed in his buckskins. With only a pistol and a serious look on his face. Whistle carried his bow across his shoulders, a quiver of arrows, and a staff with a heat-tempered point., and Fran wondered if Whistle was thinking of maybe getting close enough to use that spear.

He would only carry that one pistol, and that only for protection in an emergency. When Pino handed him his spear, Fran didn't know if he should take it or not. Pino made some hand motions, and spoke a few words that Fran didn't understand. "Take it," Charley said, "it's for you to use to find your way, not really as a weapon. You follow Whistle when you start, and he'll show you."

The lookout left in the twilight but they waited for a few minutes before leaving. "You'll have to sleep on our new bed for a little while without me," he told Angela.

"You be careful," she said, but said nothing about the bed.

They went straight across the valley, up onto the same ridge the lookout was using, Over the crest of the Whistle led Fran then turned down the shoulder just below the top, following a game trail.

The darker the night became, the more Whistle used his wooden staff. He felt his way with it, checking the trail from the ground to his head height. Under the trees, and through brushy areas, he knew when to duck under or step over what was in the trail. Fran followed that silent figure moving ahead of him. Now using the staff he'd been given the same way after watching Whistle earlier

They were dropping down toward the road when they spotted the campfire, some distance from the road, and probably not visible from it.

Whistle didn't hesitate but a minute, and then he moved on.

The camp was well hidden, their horses close by, yet Whistle made his way in close enough to hear them talking. Fran looked the camp over thoroughly. These were not an ordinary group, but an organized party. Their horses were tied next to the campsite on a picket line between trees. Their bedrolls were in a nice, straight line the way the military would set up camp. Yet the men were not dressed in any kind of uniforms. He wondered what or who these men might be.

Having seen enough, Fran pulled Whistle lightly then moved back and around toward the road, and followed along its edge heading home. There was no need for stealth any longer, with the horses and all four men in their camp.

Walking to the cabin, they found everyone waiting. Fran told them there were four men in the camp but didn't say anything about how regimented he thought the men's camp seemed.

This would be their first night in the bed he'd built, and Fran knew something had to be said about it. It would come; he was sure. "It seems higher than any bed I've slept in," Angela said.

"It is," Fran answered. "I've always had a bed I had trouble putting things under; this one I won't. Besides, I can hide under it."

The bed was accepted, their night so much nicer than on the floor.

They were not surprised in the morning when a lookout came to sit at the same tree. Fran tried to figure out, what they were looking for, or waiting for. Bart had to have, or be the answer, he figured. Except for a few miners, there had been no one interested in them being here on this stream.

When Charley and Bart came to the table, Fran thought he would tell them what he thought he saw about those four men.

"Your man up there again?" Charley asked when he sat down.

"There's a man there," Fran answered, "and, you know, there's something different about those fellows. They seem to be some kind of military men."

When he said that, he saw the slight twitch in the corner of Bart's left eye. He covered it well, but Fran knew that these men were not completely unknown to Bart. Maybe he was carrying a large amount of gold and would like to get away from here, and those men.

"You want to make a run for it, Bart? Fran asked. "I've got a horse that's not fast, but with any kind of a start he's got enough bottom to outrun most."

"I'd like to make a try," Bart answered, "but can I get by them?"

"Whistle and I can help you get by the camp, but after that you'll have to ride hard, and you'll be on your own."

"I can do it," Bart answered.

Now all Fran had to watch was that Bart didn't try to carry any, extra weight. His bay just might have to make a hard run to keep Bart out of trouble.

The work inside their cabin kept Fran busy with more pegs for them to hang their things on, and boards to be split for shelves for both cabins. He continued checking on the lookout now and then, just to make sure there was no change. When he took the horses to water, he moved the bay in close to the cabin.

Bart was helping Charley build the beds he needed in his cabin. So, Fran split more boards, knowing that both, Dove and Angela would more than likely want more shelves later on.

After lunch he went through all the rifles and pistols reloading them; then hung them on the pegs just inside the door of their cabin.

Going inside as Fran was finishing his work on the arms, Angela asked him, what was wrong.

"I was hoping it didn't show that much," he answered. But he knew just extra care with his guns alarmed her. "I am concerned about not having all the answers," he told her. "Plus, there's other things that have me wondering."

"They're an organized group, so why are they watching us? They have to want something or someone. If it's Bart or what he's carrying, they'll try going after him when he rides away tonight. That could be it, like he said."

"Can he get away?" Angela asked. "If he gets a two-minute start they'll never catch him while he's on the bay."

"Now if there's any kind of a ruckus you get everyone, and get inside the cabin." We can defend ourselves from there. It's just a precaution, Angela, and only because I don't know what I'm dealing with, but tomorrow we'll surely know one way or the other."

He watched again, waiting for the lookout to leave. Already dressed in his buckskins, he was ready, and when he saw the man leave, he went to saddle the bay, bringing the bay to where Whistle, Bart, and Charley stood away from the firelight. Fran watched as Bart loaded one small leather pouch into each saddlebag. Then as he started to tie a small bedroll behind the saddle, Fran said, "I don't think your going to need that." Sorry Bart said, it's just a habit." Fran knew Bart was nervous, and hoped that was it. "Not that it was a lot of weight, he knew the bay would be able to move, but still there was no answer about what or why, from Bart.

Dark enough to move, Fran handed Bart Pino's staff. "I'll lead the bay," Fran said. "He knows me and isn't going to fuss. You can give that back when you ride; I might need it coming home."

Straight across their valley Whistle led them, wading the stream. Then to the bottom of the rising ground and along the game trail there, then west toward the road. They followed another animal trail, near the road, that headed north. Whistle was now moving a little slower, not wanting to flush any game that might run off, alerting the men he knew were camped not all that far off.

Well past where they 'd seen the camp, Fran gave the reins of the bay to Bart, and took the staff. "Walk him a ways so they don't hear you, and then you can move out, but you'd better pace him to the distance you need to travel."

They waited until they felt Bart had a good start, and neither saw or heard any riders take after him. Retracing their route, they headed for home. Everyone was waiting except Pino, who Charley said was out checking things.

Fran had a chance to talk for a few minutes with Charley and asked him how he felt about what had been happening.

"I've been wondering myself," Charley said. "I can't figure what or why, but those boys aren't hanging around here for nothing."

Everyone went off to bed, and a night of uncertainty. "I left home," he told Angela,"because there just wasn't enough farm to support all the family. And all I've ever really wanted was a place where I could live and farm. I thought I'd found it here, but there's so much lawlessness, and no one to control it. Now I don't know if we can stay.

"We'll stay," she told him. "If they come here, we can hold the cabin. But maybe Bart had what they wanted, and they'll go after him. I don't know how he could have been carrying much, and with the start he had, they didn't have a chance of catching him."

Through she tried to comfort him, Fran spent a restless night. Up long before dawn, he was out on the veranda, looking toward the shoulder of the ridge where the lookout should appear.

The sky was just starting to lighten, and Angela had the fire burning and the coffee water on. "I'll have breakfast ready in just a few minutes."

"That will be fine," Fran answered.

The others were coming to the fire now, but everyone, even the three children, were quiet. Some how feeling the tension that they're parents, and the others were experiencing.

Chapter XIII

The sunlight had just started hitting the treetops, and then slowly descended to the ridge below. Fran kept his eye to the telescope, waiting for that figure to appear. In just a short while, as the ridge brightened with sunlight, the figure appeared. Walked to the same tree and sat down. Two minutes later Fran saw the man on his feet out on the shoulder of the ridge. The bright glints of reflected light of his telescope, now easily seen, told him the lookout was sweeping their area, looking. Not concerned now about being seen, he stayed for some time then, trotted away back toward their camp area.

Fran told Charley the lookout left after showing him self, and had surely looked them over thoroughly.

"He was looking for something," Charley said, "but what?"

"Had to be he was counting heads. They'd counted, and now they'd know there was a horse missing."

"Pretty thorough watchdogs. I wonder what we can expect next, Francis?" That was a question Fran wished he could answer.

"If it's something here," he told Charley, "it's got to be the wagon; Bart's gone."

"I checked the wagon," Charley told him. "There's nothing but a few sacks, looks like flour, cornmeal, and beans, and that's it."

Going inside, Fran buckled his second pistol on. Then slung his rifle across his back before stepping back outside, Angela, seeing the extra arms was worried, and asked, "What's wrong, Francis?"

"Nothing so far," he answered. "I just want to feel that I'm ready."

He said no more, but smiled as he left, trying to buoy her spirits a little.

They lowered the tailgate, and Charley climbed up into the wagon. "Did you look inside the stove?" Fran asked.

"Can't," Charley said, "it's all wired, and boxed shut. I tried, but I can't budge the damn thing; it's really heavy. I'll need an axe to get into it."

"Too late, Charley. They're coming; all four riders are on the road," Fran told him, as he walked toward the front of the wagon.

Charley, getting down, walked up beside him. After crossing the stream, one rider turned toward them. Then the second rider turned fifty feet past the first. Charley told Whistle to get the women and kids into the cabin. The third and fourth rider dropped off now, forming a line. "They're military, all right," Charley told Fran.

When the second man raised his arm and pointed forward, they fired their first volley, and moved forward. Out of range, the shots were lobbed in at them, only meant to perplex their enemy. Though not effective, they did drop close to the wagon and those there. "They'll keep coming like that until we either run or get hit," Charley said.

Fran, turning to Pino, put his hand out, and Pino looked puzzled but handed his staff to Fran. Kneeling, Fran, using the staff as a rest for his rifle, took aim.

"What are you going to do?" Charley asked.

"Try to take out that one giving the signals," Fran answered.

"That's a long shot, and if you miss we'd better hightail it for the cabin Francis,"

The horsemen, moving toward them, firing another volley, and Charley said, "They might charge on the next one."

Fran's rifle fired, and a second later that rider fell back off his horse. The other riders stopped, looking toward their fallen comrade, who wasn't moving.

Fran, then busy reloading, didn't see the other four riders that galloped in off the road. The first of these two of riders went after the rider that had already started back to cross the stream, trying to escape. Turning, Fran took his shot at one their other two adversaries as they were both getting off their last shots. These two then starting to make a break for it, but saw it was no use. With the four riders from the road now closing on them, and two of their cohorts already downed. They dropped both their rifles, and pistols, and sat quietly aboard their horses with their hands raised.

Fran finished with his reloading stood next to Charley and Pino watching what was now happening in front of them. "Your first shot broke their charge, Fran but it looks like somebody else is going to get to do the clean up work, Charley said. And that sure seems to be the end of it, but you keep that rifle handy anyway."

Then Bart and one of the other men rode toward them. Bart introduced, Paul Hannon, the man he told them was his boss." I thought you were an independent, Bart," Charley said.

"That's another story," Bart answered. "I'll explain later; right now I've got to walk this horse. He needs a walk and cool down." Fran's bay was lathered from running both to and from where ever Bart had gone to get his boss and the other two men.

"I'll try to clear some of this up," Paul Hannon said. "You sure deserve an explanation for what's happened here. That is Bart's wagon, but he's been doing some work for us. You see we're putting together a stage and freight line, and we're just getting started. This was a shipment that we had to move, but we didn't have a coach. We were trying to move it without anyone knowing, and this was the result. I think someone revealed our little secret, and it was probably some one from our own organization. But you can bet, I'll darn soon have that culprit. You ended up being involved, and I'm truly sorry."

"Well," Charley said, "I guess we can't find fault with you too much, but it would have been better if we'd known just a bit more."

"Everyone was sworn to secrecy," Paul told them, "including Bart."

"There's something I'd like to know though," Paul said. "Which of you took the captain out of the saddle?"

"I guess you're talking about me," Fran said. "Just figured he was their leader."

"Ex-army," Paul said. He's been a problem for us, and for a lot of others for some time now. We owe you; Thanks."

The two other men in the field left, took away the two casualties and the two prisoners, and Fran wondered but said nothing.

Paul asked Charley if they could camp there by the wagon that night. Charley told him, that he saw no reason why they couldn't.

After Bart had the bay cooled down and dry, he left off the saddle and put the bay out on a picket. When he came back he asked if Fran wanted to sell him. "I hadn't thought about it," Fran told him. "But if I did we'd be short for what I plan to do this spring, so I guess it's no."

"I'll be 'round," Bart said. "Let me know if you ever do decide."

"How are you with a pistol, Francis?" Paul asked. "We're going to need good hands when our coaches arrive."

"I guess I do all right," Fran answered. Then looking at Charley, he saw the grin on the man's face, and figured then he knew what he could expect of Francis, if the need arose.

That evening, while they were talking, Fran mentioned about their building a store. "If you build a store, add enough room for a stage stop," Paul said. "You know, a place where the passengers could stretch or get a meal."

Charley said he thought that wouldn't be all that hard to do, and would sure help in getting them started.

The two riders returned with the four horses in tow, rifles in the saddle scabbards and pistol belts hung on the saddle horns. Fran and Charley looked at each other, but both remained silent.

Bart and the two men were setting up their camp when Angela came, telling them they'd prepared enough for them, so they wouldn't have to cook. Fran introduced his wife, and Angela asked Paul if he would post a letter to Monterey. "For a meal for us, I just might deliver it myself," he said.

Angela had walked away when Charley said, "The man speaks with a bit of the blarney."

"When you talk to a beautiful young lady or the cook, it pays," Paul told them. "Plus, here I see both."

"I think I'll tell her that," Fran answered.

"You do that, Francis," Paul said. "And my congratulation to you; you really do have a most beautiful wife."

When Fran mentioned it, she told him she was flattered, and thought he was a nice man.

In the morning Angela and Dove were fixing breakfast as Paul and the others worked on Bart's wagon. They set the stove on the ground behind the wagon, with the sacks stacked on top.

They'd finished breakfast. Bart's team was in harness and their horses were saddled, when they all came over to thank the cooks and say good-bye.

"We left some things," Paul said. "We're going to have to travel fast and can't afford to carry the extra weight. That should help cover the meals we enjoyed."

"Thank you senor." Angela said. "Via con Dios."

He looked at Angela for a few seconds then told her, "I thank you senora, for being such a wonderful hostess."

They were mounting when Charley hollered, "Hey! The horses; you left the horses and saddles."

"They're yours for a job well done," Paul said, saluted, and rode toward the road.

Charley looked at Fran, and just shrugged.

The sacks they put up into the cache; then Charley hefted one end of the stove and said, "See, I knew it was full of something besides air."

Angela, looking at the stove, asked if she could have the stove on her side of the cabin. "It will be so much easier to cook on a stove like this, this winter," she said.

"You got it," Charley told her. "You are chief cook."

It was much heavier than the other stoves, but with all four of them they moved it.

They took off some parts and turned it on its side to get it in through the doorway. They set the smaller stove outside; then Charley and Whistle went to work gathering the rocks they need to level it, and lastly, install the stovepipe.

Fran and Pino carried the four saddles in, and Fran shoved them under the bed. The arms they hung on the wall, Fran knowing he'd have to clean, oil, and recharge them.

Cana and Aleta were outside by the smaller stove talking. Then they both of started talking to Whistle, and Pino, until Charley asked, "All right, what is it?"

It was Rabbit who spoke up, saying, "They want to know if you would put the stove over in your little cabin. Then, if they might move in when the cold weather comes."

"But it's so small for two families," Charley said.

"It's a whole lot bigger than the little huts, and they won't have to suffer from the smoke from the open fires," Angela pointed out.

Charley pointing to the stove and, looking at Whistle and Pino, said, "Git," and pointed toward the little cabin.

"They'll be spending most of their time over here with you anyway, Angela."

Charley went over to see if they needed any help, but Pino and Whistle had learned by working with Charley, and soon they had the stove set up. The only thing they would have to do the next day was to seal up the hole through the wall with rock and mud.

Fran, checking the horses, found them all sound, and well taken care of. Any military leader would have made sure they took care of their mounts. Walking back to the cabin, he sat at the table and then lapsed into deep thought. Seeing him there, just sitting, Angela asked if he was all right.

"I think so," Fran answered and smiled. "Just thinking about starting to build the store."

"But it's almost winter, Francis."

"I know, but if I can bring down some logs I can use some of the smaller parts of the logs to build fence; we need fenced pasture. We've got too many horses now to keep on pickets."

"Talk with Charley and see what he has to say."

"I have to do that," Fran answered.

Charley was helping Pino's families move their things and get settled in the little cabin. A woven reed mat hung in the rear gave each family a little privacy. They did have a lot more room, and the air inside wouldn't be fouled with smoke.

Charley and Fran were walking over to their cabin when Fran told Charley he wanted to start hauling timber down, and then use part of the wood for fencing.

"I guess if we're going to have a store, the sooner we start the better," Charley said, "but right now I think we need meat. And don't tell me it's my turn; you're the meat getter here. I can start laying out the building; you can go get your rifle."

"Who can I take with me, Charley?" Fran asked.

Charley said, "Your choice."

"You know I can't just pick one."

"Then have them draw straws," Charley answered.

After they finished eating supper, Fran told Whistle and Pino that he would go hunting in the morning, and one of them could go. Of course, both were eager to go. "Only one," he said, and he put two pieces of grass on the table. Pointing to the longest, he said, "This one goes," then pointing to the short one, "This one goes next time." Everyone was watching as if it was a game the two young men would play. Fran put the pieces behind his back and then brought out his hand with the pieces even above his closed fist. They both looked, but neither wanted to pick a straw. Their children were the first to coax them, and then their wives. Finally, Whistle picked a straw, and Fran gave the other to Pino.

"I go," Whistle said when they laid the straws on the table. "You go next time, Pino," Fran said. "If we don't bring something home tomorrow, Pino, you and I will go the next day after."

Angela realized that her husband, in building the store, was going to set aside what he really wanted to do, farm. She asked him if he wasn't going to do something he really didn't want to do.

"I can't start planting now; it's too early, he told her, "so, I'll build now. Come spring I'll do some planting. Right now, though, it's to go get something for our table."

"Just as long as you're happy with what you're doing, Francis, that what's important."

"And how about what you're doing?" he asked.

"I love what I'm doing. I have you, and there are our wonderful friends. What else could I want?" she told him, smiling.

Stepping outside in the morning, Fran found the fire burning and the aroma of coffee. Whistle and Cana were already up. Whistle must be anxious, Fran thought. With the first light he walked out to bring in the horses he'd saddle—one packhorse and the two horses they'd ride.

Angela packed them each a lunch as they ate the breakfast Cana had prepared.

Fran tightened the cinch on the horse Whistle would ride. He took his staff, and held the horse as Whistle mounted. Though Fran knew how inexperienced Whistle was, he was surprised when he saw him spring up onto the saddle, and he knew that Whistle had been watching others mount. Handing him the reins and his staff, Fran adjusted the stirrups. His own cinch tightened, he'd kissed Angela, slung the rifle she held out to him over his shoulder, and mounted. "Early this afternoon if we're lucky," he told her.

They rode west toward the lower, flat, valley lands, the tulle lands, streams and ponds, willow along the streams, and large oaks on the drier areas. As they moved to follow the trails made by the animals, Fran let Whistle lead. For an hour they moved mostly west; finally, Whistle stopped, and dismounted, but not the way most did. Whistle had swung his right leg over the saddle horn, then dropped to ground on quiet moccasined feet, as silent as a cat. Fran smiled; he knew that Whistle, like many of the Indians, would become an excellent horseman, like the vaqueros from the missions and ranchos.

Their horses picking on grass, Fran followed Whistle along a game trail, always trying to step where Whistle stepped, trying to be as quiet as he could. He saw the tracks of the animal they'd come after, and was sure Whistle would be doing his best to help him get a shot.

Whistle would stop and listened every once in a while, but was soon stopping more often, and chirping like a bird. Fran wondered why, and was even more surprised when he heard the answering chirps.

The breeze that came from out of the west kept their scent from any animal ahead. Soon he heard the chirping sound coming from more than one area ahead of them. Then once in a while he heard the crack of a stick or small limb breaking. Whistle came to a stop just before the trail broke out into a small clearing. Fran looked to where he pointed, and there just on the other side of the clearing looking toward them, stood a spike bull elk. Raising his rifle slowly, he fired. The shot sent other animals crashing off through the brush, and Fran realized then, that it wasn't a bird that made that chirping noise.

They walked to the downed animal, both smiling. They had what they came after, and three or four times the meat they would get from a single deer.

Fran asked, "Whistle, that chirp, chirp noise?"

Whistle, a broad grin, pointed to the downed animal, and said, "Him;" then pointing toward where the other animals ran, he said, "Him too." And Fran then knew for sure that as large as these animals were, they chirped like a bird. Whistle had chirped too, making the animals think it was other animals behind them.

Whistle was already positioning the animal to remove its insides, hooking one of the animal's back legs behind a bush. Leaving his rifle, Fran trotted back to where they'd left the horses. Bringing them back to where they'd need them now. As he got close to where Whistle had downed the elk, the horses balked, and snorted, not liking the smell of what was there. He knew it wasn't just the smell of blood because they didn't act this way when they were around the deer he'd butchered.

These horses didn't like the odor of the elk themselves. Easy enough to understand why, he said to himself, some of these animals were almost as large as a small horse. Then of course there were those big bull elk with their large antlers that even a large stallion would have little chance against.

Whistle had the elk skinned on its own hide, they could start cutting the animal up, and loading the pack bags. It was too much for the packhorse alone, so Fran would carry some meat, and Whistle rolled up the hide and would carry it behind his saddle. They washed up in a nearby pond, ate their lunch, and were ready to head home. The going home would be slow, but if they didn't have any problems they make it easily, before dark.

They had drifted a little north of the route they had taken coming out, trying to stay away from the wet, soft areas with the heavily loaded horses.

The horses were the first to pick up the smell, and they started acting up, shaking their heads, and snorting. When Fran caught the smell of rotting flesh, he knew why the horses were disturbed. They were fairly close to whatever it was, and he waved to Whistle to wait where they were. That he would go on foot to check. He made his way through about forty yards of brush before the clearing. There, what he saw almost made him sick. He hurried back to his horse mounted, and motioned to Whistle to head for home.

Greeted there by a happy bunch seeing as how they'd been successful. Most of the meat they'd hoist up into the cache, with the liver and heart kept for their evening meal. The women stretched the elk hide while the men worked hoisting the meat. Fran and Whistle cared for the horses as the women, finishing with the hide, began cooking supper.

Coming back, Fran asked if there was hot water; he'd like to bathe. Looking at her husband, Angela knew there was something wrong, but she didn't ask.

CHAPTER XIV

Bathed, Fran sat down across the table from Charley and asked if Charley would take a walk after they'd eaten. "All right," Charley answered, but he wondered what was bothering Francis and why he didn't want to talk around the others.

When they'd finished supper, Charley told Fran they should walk down and check out where he'd set the stakes. Almost dark, he said, "but you can get an idea." As they started walking, Charley asked Fran what was on his mind. "I found them," Fran said. "And who's *them*?" Charley asked.

"The four men who came at us and Paul Hannon's men took away."

"Charley, they hung the two who were alive, and just dumped the other two."

Charley walked on a ways before he said anything. Then he said, "Fran, I'm afraid that's the way it's going to be here for a while. They took those fellas out that way, because there just was no other way. And you remember Francis; those men knew what they doing, and what would happen if they got caught.

"You just think, Francis, what would have happened if we had given in to those four. What would have happened to you and me, then the women, and then the kids? Then, when they did what they wanted, they would have burned what they didn't want, and we'd be left to rot in the sun. Harsh way to put it, I know but for now that's the way it's gonna be."

"It's about as bad here as it is in Yerba Buena," Fran told' Charley, "just less people."

"It looks big," he told Charley when he saw the stakes where Charley marked the perimeter outline of the store. "Probably be all right to start with," Charley answered, "but it's really not that big when you figure part is living quarters." They walked back in the dark and sat down at the table with coffee.

"I might as well start tomorrow," Fran said. "It's going to take a lot of logs to put that place together."

"You start on the logs; I'll start hauling rock," Charley answered. The night air was cold now; everyone else had gone inside. They finished their coffee, said there good night, and retired inside.

Angela was waiting for him, standing by the stove. Where she'd just built a fire to take the chill out of the cabin. Fran went by the bed and started undressing.

"You going to bed?" she asked.

"I'm a little tired," he answered, "it's been a long day."

"Are you all right, Francis?"

"I'm all right now; I've just got to learn to be a little more callous about some things."

"I like you the way you are, Francis. I don't want to see you become hard and cruel like those men who came here."

With the weather colder, they cooked on the larger stove inside, keeping the cabin warm for the children. Fran, Pino, and Whistle worked falling and trimming the logs for the store. Charley worked at the building site and kept his eye on their camp.

Fran selected the trees that they could best use. Those too large they would pass, even though they could use some of the tops of the trees. They figured forty logs for the walls; these they'd drag down first. Later they would get the tops and heavier limbs, which they could use for fencing or firewood.

Stormy days they stayed in their cabins sharpening their tools and repairing their leather harness, which had taken a lot of punishment while they worked in the wet.

Another hunt was needed, and this time Pino would go, but this time Fran would take two packhorses, not wanting to overtax any of their animals. Again Fran followed a bird-chirping guide, and he had to smile. It was another close shot in some brushy cover but this time a larger animal, and he was glad he had brought the second packhorse, knowing if he hadn't they'd have to pack their mounts and walk back home. Even with the two packhorses, they had heavy loads. Pino was smiling all the time he worked, happy they had plenty of meat now, and it would keep well in the cool.

Fran knew now about what it must have been like when Pino and Whistle hunted with only their bows. They might have to follow the blood trail of an arrow-hit animal a long ways. Then, with this much meat, they'd have to move their families to the site and camp while they smoke-cured most of the animal.

It had been a good and successful hunt, and now Pino, like Whistle, insisted they pack everything, even the head and antlers. They had a use for almost every part of the animal.

Fran led the way home, staying away from that place he didn't care to see again. He looked back at Pino bringing up the rear; a somewhat happy, but really more of a satisfied look on the Indian's face.

It was snowing lightly as they approached the cache, and they'd go through the same routine getting the meat up into the cache and taking care of the horses. Cana and Aleta took care of the children while Dove and Angela had the liver plus wild onions on the stove. Always seeming to be their favorite meal, after a successful hunt of either a deer or an elk. Everyone was in the one cabin, keeping warm while they ate. "Let 'er snow," Charley said. "We're all set for a month."

Everyone left not long after supper; their stoves would need to be stoked. Angela had water on their stove, knowing Fran liked to bathe after spending a day out hunting. He put the bar across the door, knowing no one ever knocked, and he would be out in the middle of the room bathing, or he could get caught stoking the stove with no clothes on in the morning.

They were warm, the night was quiet, and they talked for a little while; Fran told Angela he just had to plant something when the weather warmed. "I've got to find out how well things will grow here," he said.

He got up in a cold cabin, no fire now only a few coals. He put in a few small sticks, then heavier pieces on top. Then went and took the bar off the door. Running back he got into bed, cuddling up close to Angela, who was warm and soft and felt so nice next to him.

"You took the bar off the door, Francis. Someone might come in."

'I don't care," he answered. "I'm not getting up to put the bar back."

"You might be embarrassed, my husband."

"No," he answered. "They'll be embarrassed, but I'll be happy."

They were up and dressed, and Angela had the water on for coffee when they heard the knock. A heavy hand and a loud knock, they knew it could only be one person, Charley.

"It don't look like we'll get much done today," he said. "There's snow on the ground."

"You got coffee, Angela?"

"In a minute," she answered. "Sit down, Charley, you can talk to Francis about planting this spring."

Charley asked what he had planned?

"Not too much," Fran told him. "Turning the ground by hand isn't going to give me a chance to plant a lot, just some corn, beans, and squash."

"That's an Indian way to plant those three," Charley said. "Some of the eastern tribes use it. They plant three or four corn kernels on a mound. When the corn gets a foot or so tall, you plant a bean at each corn plant. Then when the beans start growing up those corn stalks, you plant your squash seed. The squash plants shade the ground and keep it from drying out some."

Fran smiled. "If it worked for them, I don't see why it wouldn't work here, for us," he said

"There is one other thing, though," Charley said. "They put a fish in each mound for their corn God."

"Guess I'll have to skip that part," Fran said. "I haven't got fish one."

"Course there's the corn dance too," Charley said, laughing. "But if your harvest is good, we might all dance."

The coffee ready, they sat with the cups as the others trickled in for breakfast. After the horses were cared for, it was back to the cabins warmth. It was the first day they'd had to really rest, but they were bored. It would be siesta for them also, after the children were put down for their nap. Then after supper they'd all retire early.

The next day would be different; that morning, after breakfast, the four men were going down to work. The rock for the foundation in place, they could start splitting logs for the floor.

With a large fire built with the scraps, they could warm up between stints of work. Every day now they worked, determined to get the store built; spring would mean a new surge of men coming in search of their fortune. Those men would require not only food but also tools and hardware.

With the roof on, the women helped with the chinking of the logs. But when Charley mentioned that there would be some work to do on some other type of houses, the ladies declined the invitation. That was work for the men, they told him.

The covered veranda in front plus the covered deck in the back would require split logs, lumber, and shingles. All of it was heavy work with axe, adz, and splitting mall.

They didn't have glass for the windows and would have to wait until Bart started his freight wagon hauling in the spring. For now, they'd just put the shutters on.

With most of the work done on the building, Charley concentrated on building furniture, counters, and shelves they'd need, while Fran worked turning the soil for the garden. This was the best and easiest time to do it, but it was still hard, backbreaking work.

The work running out inside, Pino and Whistle started helping Fran. Their next chore would be the fences and cleaning up the wood debris where they worked the logs for the store, the fence posts, and rails. Charley was driving stakes to mark the lane every afternoon, walking up for supper.

If it were to rain hard, they'd have to stay in all day. Charley was troubled now, telling Angela that Dove had been ill but wouldn't tell him anything, other than she didn't feel well. "Plus," he said, those other two are closemouthed; they're not talking either."

Angela found Cana and Aleta with Dove, but Dove was sitting up, smiling, and said she was all right now. "You've been sick for a few days Dove," Angela said. "What is it?" Dove started to cry then, and Angela knew Dove was with child.

"Are you going to have a child?" Angela asked, and Dove pleaded, "Please don't tell Charley, He'll send me away."

"*No*, he won't send you away, Dove," Angela said, "I promise you."

"I'm afraid," Dove insisted and wouldn't stop crying.

Angela tried to comfort her. But in her own mind Angela knew that there were men who did feel this way but, no, not Charley; she knew he wasn't that kind of man. Back at her cabin, she found the four men sitting at the table. As Charley looked up Angela said, "She needs you, Charley."

"She needs me?" Charley asked.

"Go comfort her, Charley. She's worried about how you'll feel about becoming a father."

At first a look of shocked surprise was on Charley's face. Then there was a smile as he stood and left the room.

A minute later, Cana and Aleta came in saying Charley had told them to leave. It was awhile before they walked in, Charley holding Dove close and walking her to the table to sit down. "I can help with supper, Charley," Dove said. "I'll be fine now."

Fran, Whistle, and Pino were all looking at him, smiling, when Charley looked over at them. "I might be old," he said, "but I ain't that old yet."

"Congratulations, Charley," Fran said.

"You think I deserve that, Francis?" Charley asked.

"Why not, Charley? You did have something to do with it."

"I guess I did, but you know, I know nothing about being a father."

"You'll do fine, Charley," Angela said. "Just keep doing what you've been doing with Rabbit."

"Him and me," he told them, "are good friends; it ain't like I'm being his pa."

"But that's what a boy's father is, Charley. He's a boy's best friend," Angela told him.

Back at work, their days were concentrated in and around the store, though Fran did take time to show Whistle and Pino how to use the rifles, so they could shoot on their hunts, but he kept the rifles near his and Angela's room at the store.

Angela's stove now installed in the store's kitchen, and a dinning area, a place where they could all come, and eat together.

Whistle and Pino moved the stove from the smaller cabin, and they and their families would share the larger cabin now, next to Charley, Dove, and Rabbit.

Bart's first load was window glass, and the things Charley had ordered; now the store was taking shape. Four days later, four Mexican horsemen and a dozen pack mules were in front of the store. Miguel came in and told Charley he was looking for his sister, Angela, and brother-in-law, Francis Leon. Angela heard her brother's voice and came running out to meet him; Rabbit ran out the back door, going to tell Fran that he had visitors. Surprised to find Miguel here, Fran wondered how he'd been able to find them.

After welcoming Miguel and the other riders, Fran helped them take their pack animals to the rear of the store. They removed the loads from the animals and then went back inside, where Angela had a meal fixed for her brother and the other riders.

Now Fran got to see the map that Miguel said Angela sent with the letter to her father. "Followed it right to this spot," Miguel said, "but I didn't expect to see the store already built."

Giving Fran the list of items they brought, the cost of each one. "All you have to do is figure your markup," he said.

"How did he know what to send?" Fran asked.

"Papa sent the same things everyone was buying there when they headed this way," Miguel said.

Fran gave the list to Charley to look at. "My partner, Charley," he told Miguel.

"That's about half the price Bart has been charging us," Charley said. "How much do we owe Miguel?"

"Papa used some of the money Francis left with him; everything is paid for," Miguel said.

Angela sat and talked to her brother and the others for a few minutes. She asked how long they would stay. "We'll leave in about five minutes," Miguel said. "We can see there will be no fiestas here. Our job is done; we can stop at the mission for one night's fiesta there, and then home."

Angela smiled and said, "All right, little brother. I wouldn't want you and your friends to miss too many nights." She gave him a letter to her father and the family and said, "Be careful; this is not a very peaceful country."

They left a guitar on the table, Miguel saying, "We brought your guitar, sister."

"Thank you, little brother. I've missed it."

Miguel, kissing his sister's cheek, said, "We'll be back again soon."

Everyone went out to bid the riders via con Dios. Fran remembered watching these young men dance at the nightly fiestas in Monterey. But now he wondered why they seemed so different. They were out of sight when everyone walked back inside. Fran stopped by the table, thinking, and Angela asked him if there was something wrong. "There's something about your brother and the others that's different," Fran said." They're on horseback now," Angela said. "Maybe that's it."

"No, it's the pistols, Angela. They're all armed. No one in Monterey carried arms when I were there. I wonder if they have to carry arms there now, or was it just for the trail?

"Things are changing, Francis. We can't do much about it."

Charley, standing by Fran, had heard everything. "She's right, Francis," he said. "We can only watch out for our own little bailiwick. We've already had a taste of it, now, like those young fellas wearing sidearms, we had better be ready."

For the next couple of days, Charley, Angela, Cana, and Aleta would keep busy unpacking, pricing, and putting the new stock in place. Dove took care of the children back near the kitchen while Fran, Whistle, and Pino worked outside on the fence and in the garden area.

Riders moved along the road now, though it was still muddy in places. But it was drying fast. Some of the riders stopped to see what the store had to offer. Most were looking for something stronger to drink, than what Charley told them he had to offer. Charley did sell some things, and he knew he would sell more. Mainly because most of the men who came here, were not equipped for what they were going after.

Their midday meal finished, Fran, Whistle, and Pino brought the arms that Fran had been keeping to the store. Whistle and Pino each would keep a rifle for hunting, but neither wanted a pistol. Fran hung his rifle over the door in the bedroom along with a second pistol. Two rifles were just outside the door along with two pistols, plus the possibles bags and powder horns. The other rifles and pistols they hung behind the counter, where Charley could sell them.

The pistol Fran carried every day, he would hang by the bed at night, and Angela's pistol he hung up high in the pantry. She was watching him apprehensively, and when he turned he saw the look on her face. "It's just a precaution," he said. "You'll probably never need it." In his own mind Fran knew there was a good chance that she might, but he prayed it would never happen.

With the larger stove now in the kitchen at the store, Dove, Aleta, and Cana moved their daily work there behind the store. Their grinding stones were under a new shelter and another horno built so they could bake their bread. Everyone was taking their meals here now, using the kitchen, but their table was away from the tables for customers, if they ever came.

They were working on the fence when Fran saw the stage and told Pino and Whistle, "It's getting close to noon; we'll quit now and go see what the stage brings in." After washing, Fran had just walked through the door when he heard a man's loud, gruff voice ask, "Where the hell's the bar."

Then Charley answered, "Sorry, mister, we don't serve liquor here; this is a family business."

"You fellas sit down. I'll get a bottle from the stage," Fran heard the man say.

Then Charley answered, "Please don't bring it in here. If you want to eat, fine. But no liquor."

Fran lifted the thong off the hammer of his pistol and walked into the dining area, taking a quick look at the three men at the table, and the man standing just inside the front door. That man, he figured, would be the one looking for a problem. This was a big man ,with big hands, and fat fingers. His holster, though tied down, was set far forward on his hip. He was a powerful bear of a man but probably not a man quick with a pistol. He was looking straight at Fran now and had to see that he was facing, a young man well armed. And definitely, a decidedly different adversary than the older man, who stood unarmed behind the counter.

The guard from the stage pushed the big man aside as he came through the door, his coach gun slung over his right shoulder. "Go sit down and enjoy your meal," the guard said. "Any more trouble from you, and you can walk from here." One of the other men at the table spoke up as Dove walked in with the small, hand-written menu. "Keep that blabbermouth of yours shut, Don," the guard said,' I've heard enough from you already, and I don't want to hear anymore, understand?"

They were served elk steak rubbed with chili, beans, fresh bread or a large stack of hot tortillas, coffee, and acorn cookies.

After they had eaten, one of the other men spoke up from the table, telling the others. "You guys pay for your meal, and leave a decent tip. That was the most reasonably priced meal we've had on this trip. And that goes for you too, Don. Understand?"

Walking over to where Charley and Fran stood, the man said, "I'm sorry about him. He's a good hand at moving gravel at our claim, and he's a strong man if he can get his hands on you, but he's a fool, that can't use a pistol. Thanks for a good meal at a fair price; you're the first that hasn't gouged us. We're fairly close, so we'll be back to do some shopping, now and then. And I'll see he's kept away." Turning to Fran he said, "And you, young fella, keep that pistol of yours well oiled. This country's going to need some like you. You'll be the ones who are going to be called on to keep the riffraff down to a minimum."

Charley and Fran stood side by side as the stage pulled out and, continued watching until it was out of sight. When they turned face to face, Charley asked, "Well, Francis, what do you think."

"I'm really not happy about what happened, Charley," Fran answered. "I don't like that kind of responsibility."

Charley just looked at Fran for a second, then, put his arm around his shoulder. He knew there was nothing he could really say and knew it could more than likely happen again, and they'd be in the middle of it. Gold had brought the good, and the bad to California. There were those who would work the streams, and earth for that yellow metal. Then the others, who'd look for ways to extract it from those lucky enough to have found it. Honest merchants and traders, yes, but others who looked for easier, more devious and dishonest ways to get their gold. The one's who would rob, steal or even kill for it. Plus that faction that neither he nor Fran could fathom. The ones who'd without compunction kill any Indian, Mexican, or Chinese man, woman, or child. The man they had called Don was one of these, he was sure. Fran knew, he had seen the hate in the man's eyes when Dove came into the dining area.

But he'd keep this to himself, knowing what it would do to Charley and the others.

CHAPTER XV

The stage came back the next day carrying two men who had sold their claims and were heading home, and Fran wondered if they'd make it safely.

It was too early to quit for their midday meal, so Fran, with Pino and Whistle, kept at their work. Rabbit came out to tell Fran that Charley wanted him inside. "Might just as well quit for lunch," Fran told Pino and Whistle. But as they walked toward the rear of the store he wondered why he was needed.

Inside, Charley told him, "The stage driver wanted to know if he talked the stage company into it, would we be willing to take care of a change of horses here?

"It would mean a monthly stipend for a stock tender, who'd have to cut hay, but they'd furnish the grain."

"I can talk to Whistle and Pino; they could split the work and the money. That would give them something to spend. I sure wouldn't be able to, when there's hunting that work has still got to be done."

Pino and Whistle were agreeable. In fact, they were glad that they would be able to earn some cash, and one or the other of them was always there.

But now Fran would have to see to fencing off a corral and then building a place to store grain where the mice and raccoons couldn't get to it—a cache of sort but lower than their other one. Another water trough would take him a day to build with the tools and material he had.

Fran, Whistle, and Pino worked for over a week on the project, even building a pole barn shelter for the horses, with a loft for hay storage.

It was Sunday morning, and Fran, getting out of bed, told Angela to put on her riding britches, that they were taking a ride. Smiling, she asked, "Shall I pack a lunch?"

"You'd better," he told her, "if you want to eat."

He had their horses saddled and tied at the rear of the store when Charley came to open. "About time you took a day off," Charley said.

"And you?" Fran asked.

"The store's like a holiday every day for me," Charley said. "It's the easiest I've ever had it, and I like what I'm doing."

"You be careful where you ride, Francis," Charley told them as they went into the rear of the store. Inside, Fran sat at the table watching Angela make breakfast, and he smiled. She had never asked to take one minute off or complained about how hard she had to work. He knew he had taken her away from a comfortable, easy, and pleasant life in Monterey. He now wondered if she ever regretted leaving there. She smiled when she brought him coffee and asked, "Why so somber, mi amor?"

"Just thinking," he answered, and let it end there. She walked back to the stove, and he felt somewhat guilty. *We could have stayed there*, he thought.

Dove, Aleta, and Cana came in talking and laughing in their native language, but changed quickly into English when they saw Fran. They quickly took over the kitchen as Angela brought breakfast, and sat down.

He could tell she was happy, actually elated, about taking this ride, and he a felt a little better.

She picked up the dishes, saying, "I'll see you out side in a minute." He was putting his rifle into the saddle scabbard when she came out buckling on her pistol belt. He watched as she tied her holster down, and checked the thong over the pistol's hammer. She was ready to ride. "Where's the lunch?" he asked.

"I forgot it," she said.

When she was turning to go back, Dove handed the bag to her.

The three magpies stood and watched as they rode toward the road. Looking back, Fran saw Pino and Whistle walking toward the store with the children all waving.

Out on the road, they headed north across the stream, then up through the grass meadow toward the higher ground. Following the game trails, they rode single file until reaching the first hilltop. Here, most of the time, they could ride side by side.

It was a pleasant, warm, spring day; the first wildflowers were in bloom, and squirrels were scolding from the canopy above.

An occasional deer would rise from its bed, trot off a short distance, and then stop and look back at the horses. Unafraid of this unfamiliar four-legged animal, the horse, but unaware that the two-legged animal they feared was there also. Once they scented man, they quickly lengthened their stride and sped off.

Another hour of riding, and the ridge they followed curved east. They rode out into a grassy slope, from where they could look west toward their back trail and out into the expanse of the valley. The store and cabin were hidden from their view by the height of the ridges, and the trees below.

After putting their horses on pickets, Fran took the blanket he brought and spread it out on the slope. "It's a nice place for a picnic," Angela said as she brought their lunch and canteen.

They ate the lunch and took turns using Fran's telescope to look out over the vast valley, the Mexicans called San Joaquin and the river with the same name. "There could be a thousand farms out there," he said, "it's all so big."

"I'm sure there will be one day," Angela answered.

Their lunch finished, they were lying back and looking up at a clear blue sky. He moved closer to her, kissed her, and pulled the blanket over them. "Here? Now?" Angela asked.

"No," he asked.

"I'd never deny you, Francis, remember that."

They were lying close, looking at the sky again. Angela kissed him and said, "Thank you, Francis."

"For what we just did?" he asked.

"No, not just that," she said. "For loving me."

"You don't have to thank me for that. It's my pleasure, my love," and he returned her kiss. Holding each other, in the warmth had made them sleepy.

He might have dozed off. He didn't know, but the horses had quit cropping the new grass; everything was too quiet. Rolling over, he pulled one of his pistols from its holster, laying it beside him. Then, as he looked out past the horses, and only a few hundred feet away, he saw it.

"What is it?" Angela asked as she was hurriedly dressing.

"Look right over there, a little way in front of the horses."

Rolling over to look, she said, "Coyote, but an awfully large one."

Still in his darker winter coat, the coyote was large and beautiful. He just sat looking right at them, like he was interested. Both ears were up, and he cocked his head from side to side now and then.

"I bet he'd run off if I stood up," Fran said.

"Anyone would," Angela said, laughing, "if you stood up like that, with no clothes on."

"Oh, you know what I mean," he answered.

The coyote finally stood up, turned, and trotted away; he looked back one time then disappeared into the timber. "They're almost as big as a wolf up here in these mountains," Fran said. "I guess they have to be; it must be tough living up here in the winter."

Picking up, they mounted, and rode south. Fran figured they'd ride down on the opposite side of their little valley. He knew the ridge well and knew it would be easier on the horses.

They could see the cabins, and the store when they were above the little hidden hollow where Pino and Whistle, with their families, had lived. The huts were still there, and Fran, reining in his horse, stopped. "What is it?" Angela asked.

"I thought I saw a wisp of smoke," he answered.

They sat for a few minutes before they saw a figure move from one hut to the other. "Pretty good fire," Fran said. "There's hardly any smoke; they mustn't want anyone to know they're here."

Taking out his telescope, he dismounted and sat watching the huts until the figure moved again. "I figured they were Indians," he said, getting up. I wonder how long they've been hiding out there. They've had a tough winter someplace, you can be sure."

On down to the road then, they rode past the store to the stream to let their horses drink. Then went to the rear of the store, where Angela got off, letting Fran take the horses off to care for them.

In their kitchen, Angela asked the other women if they knew there were people living in the huts up in the hidden hollow. They didn't, and Angela could only tell them what she saw, only the one person. The three girls knew it could only be some of their people; now they wondered, who.

They wouldn't say anything now; they'd let the men talk things over at suppertime. But they did fix extra food just in case Charley would send Whistle and Pino to check, and they were sure he would.

When Fran came in, he went straight to the front of the store to tell Charley what he saw at the huts. "Guess we'd better send Whistle and

Pino up to take a check, "Charley said. "They'd just run off if either of us went."

"I'll get Angela to get something for them to eat," Fran said.

"Yeah," Charley answered. "I'm sure they're probably half starved."

Meeting Pino and Whistle at the rear of the store when they came in for their evening meal, he told them.

They hadn't been up near the huts, and didn't know anyone was there. They wanted to leave right then to go check, but Fran told them to wait. After they had eaten, then they could take some food for whoever was there.

"Check and see who they are, I'm pretty sure they're some of your people," Fran said. "Then you hustle back and tell Charley what you found; he'll figure out what to do."

Fran watched as Pino and Whistle trotted up the slightly rising ground toward the cabins then disappeared into the hidden hollow. Charley and Fran sat at the table drinking coffee for the better part of an hour; the women were all in the kitchen talking. Pino and Whistle came in rather somber and sat down.

"Well?" Charley asked.

"They're skinny, ragged, and dirty," Whistle said, "almost staved; they've been hiding out up in the caves. An old man and his wife, their daughter, her husband, and their little girl."

Charley sat for a minute; Dove came to sit next to him. Looking at Whistle and Pino, Charley said, "tomorrow you two take the tub over to the little cabin and heat water for those men to bathe in. Take some clothes from the store; make sure they're plenty big. Those men will put on weight fast with food in their bellies. Cana, Aleta, you do the same with the women, and then move them into the cabin.

"After you can teach them English, I don't want to see them down here near the store until they learn, hear me. The same people who've been raising havoc with them up in the hills will more than likely be coming by the store. Speaking English will afford them some protection, and we'll have to give them the rest."

Dove laid her head on Charley's shoulder and said, "You're a good man, my husband. I hope I can give you a son."

"You already have," Charley said, "Rabbit my right-hand helper around the store." Which Rabbit was, always trying to help Charley with things he could do, mostly sweeping the store and the boardwalk out front.

Charley, talking to Pino and Whistle, told them to clean out the little cabin. "Bring the saddles and bridles here to the store," he said. "Everything else you can put up in the cache for now." After they had left, he talked with Fran, telling him he thought another hunt would be needed soon.

Fran had just started working in the garden when Bart pulled in with a stage team in tow.

There was half a wagonload of goods for the store, and half his load was grain for the stage teams. Laying his hoe against the nearby fence, Fran went over to give Bart a hand. With Pino and Whistle working on the cabin, it would be up to him and Bart to take care of the work of unloading. The horses taken care of and the grain unloaded, Bart moved his wagon to the rear of the store, where they unloaded the rest. They carried everything in to where Charley could check them against his order, knowing there would usually be some items missing, and he'd have to reorder. "How come," he asked Bart, "I can never get everything I order?"

"I gather up what I can," Bart answered. "If they don't have it I can't get it; maybe next time."

It was close to noon before they finished, so Fran and Charley sat and listened as Bart brought them up to date on the news. "Things are about the same," he said. "San Francisco burns every few months, and they murder some most days. Sacramento's been a church social compared to the old Yerba Buena. There's been about the usual killings, and a few hangings in the gold camps, and the settlements, some holdups too. There's always someone what figures it's a lot easier to get gold after someone else has worked it out of the ground. And some of them are working together in small gangs."

Fran saw the look on Charley's face and knew that what Bart had just told them, bothered him. He knew too that they could find themselves targets of these groups of men. Their vulnerability was so prevalent; he remembered what he went through when he exited that place they now called San Francisco.

They sat on the benches they'd made for stage passengers out in front of the store. Charley was working on their order when Dove came out to tell them that lunch was on the table.

Inside, they continued their talks, Charley saying he figured their business would be slow for a while. Many of the miners just getting back to their claims would have purchased supplies from the town where they'd spent their winter.

Charley paid Bart and asked if he wasn't a bit leery about carrying cash with him. "I only keep some pocket money on me," Charley said, "the rest I rat hole where they ain't got a chance of finding it." Charley didn't ask him where his rat hole was, but he did remind him that the two small stoves he ordered he'd expect delivered before next winter.

Bart left, and Fran went back out to work in the garden; he didn't last long. It was getting too hot. Right now he'd take a siesta; later he'd work for a few hours in the cooler late afternoon.

Inside, as he sat down, Angela came to sit with him. They had barely gotten seated when Rabbit, with Bonita and Chico, came running in, laughing. Oblivious of the heat of the day, they said they ran ahead of the grown-ups and wondered if they could have chocolate before everyone sat down to talk. With a smile, Angela went to the kitchen to make chocolate for the children.

When Whistle and Pino came in, they carried four woven reed bowls. Gifts, they said, from the others for letting them stay in the cabin. They said they knew it wasn't much and would have liked to do more, but it was all they had.

Charley put the bowls up in the store where their customers could see them. Then he told Whistle, "You and Pino get seed from Angela and then go show them where and how to plant a garden. They can raise food for themselves and sell whatever they have extra.

For the next week, Charley kept busy in the store; Fran worked in their garden while Pino and Whistle worked helping with the new garden up by the cabins. Cana and Aleta worked helping the women with their work and were teaching them English, like Charley wanted. Dove and Angela took care of the kitchen, cooking all the meal for them. Also, they prepared the meals for the people who stopped in off the stage, which now stopped four times a week, stopping both times, going south then stopping again when it headed back north.

Charley told Fran at supper he was sure getting tired of salted meat with beans. "Some red meat would be good for all of us, Francis," he said, "and you could use a day away from that hoe." Looking at Pino and Whistle, Fran saw the smiles; they knew one of them would also get to go. It was time to draw straws. Whistle got up from their table and went outside, coming back in a minute with a single long stem of dry grass. He handed the grass stem to Fran, who passed it to Charley, saying, "You're the patriarch here; you get the honor." Pino got the long straw, but Whistle just shrugged, knowing the next hunt would be his. "Two packhorses,

Pino," Fran said, "just in case we get a good-size bull; we don't want to take a cow this time of year." They knew most cows would be nursing their new calves.

The bulls would have shed their antlers, and it was going to be difficult to tell a bull from a cow.

Both Pino and Whistle were there before first light, ready for an early breakfast. They'd wait after eating until full light before they got ready the horses.

Fran got their rifles, his pistol, their other gear, and lunch. By then, Whistle had the horses at the rear of the store. Fran kissed Angela; they mounted and waved to Charley, Dove, Aleta, Cana, Rabbit, Chico, and Bonita as they were coming down for breakfast. Out around the end of the store they went, across the road, and then they rode straight east, down toward the tulle thickets and oak meadows. Pino led the way, knowing where he wanted to hunt, while Fran followed with the packhorses. This was Pino's hunt, and Fran was satisfied in letting him do it as he pleased. They rode for two hours. Then Pino stopped where they'd leave the horses.

When Pino started off to make his stalk, Fran lagged behind, just barely keeping Pino in sight, trying not to make any noise and spoil Pino's hunt. Fran enjoyed listening to the birdlike chirps Pino made and then hearing the elk make the same birdlike chirps. When Pino stopped, Fran did too. He stood still, just watching. Even after Pino shot, he waited until he had seen him reload. Then, when Pino moved, he followed.

When Fran got to Pino, he was already working with his knife. He helped him until they had the animal gutted before he went back to get the horses. The horses had to be left at some distance away from the elk; all horses seemed to have that aversion when they knew by smell or sight that another animal was near, dead or alive.

They skinned this animal just as they had the others. They removed the leg and shoulder bones then the meat from the backbone, and they sawed off the ribs. The only bones to carry away would be the ribs and the neck. Once they had the meat packed, they stopped and ate their lunch. Twenty minutes later the packs and hide were loaded, and they were ready for the homeward trek.

Chapter XVI

Stopping at the first stream they came to, they let the horses drink, and washed the blood off their hands, arms, and tools.

Pino led off for their ride home with a smile on his face. Fran knew he was proud of what he'd accomplished, having just bagged they're largest bull elk so far. He deserved that right, Fran felt. Having watched both Pino and Whistle exercise their skills hunting, and he was proud knowing them.

They rode through the heat of the afternoon, wanting to get the meat home as fast as possible, knowing they had to process the meat quickly or risk losing the food, plus the time and labor they had just expended.

Following the same trail they came out on, it would take them longer now because of the loads the packhorses were carrying.

Breaking out into the open, they could see the road ahead, the store, and the three horses at the hitching rail. Two horses were tied to it, and one horse with a rider aboard. Fran figured that two of the three were inside buying their supplies while that man waited. Pino led the way up to the store as that man watched them. They moved off the road, going past the end of the store toward the rear. They'd just moved out of view of the man on horseback when Fran heard the whistle. That whistle, he knew, could be a signal, and he unslung his rifle from across his back. He brought his left leg over the horn of his saddle and dropped to the ground, releasing the reins and ground reining his horse.

Moving toward the front of the store, he carried his rifle in his right hand. At the corner of the building he was only able to see no more than the leg of the mounted rider, and he moved toward the outer edge of the covered deck. As he moved he saw another man exiting the store carrying sacks; he reached the edge of the deck, the man tossed the mounted man two of the sacks. As that man dropped the sacks in front of his saddle, he saw Fran. Making eye contact, he dropped his hand to his pistol. Fran knew he couldn't beat the man with the first shot and knew he had little protection from the roof's corner post he stood by, but he brought his rifle up. He saw the bright blossom from the pistol, felt the tug on his shirt, and the burn as the lead cut a furrow along his side.

His rifle bucked, and he saw the man go over backwards off his horse, and the horse danced side ways out into the road. The second man now fought to get clear of the other two sacks he carried and reach his pistol. Dropping his rifle, Fran knew he could beat this man to the draw; things were moving fast as he heard the shot, and then heard Angela scream. A third man was backing out of the doorway of the store. Charley's cash box in his left hand, and his pistol in his right. The man fired again into the store and was turning toward him as he fired at the man with the sacks.

Fran was swinging toward the third man, trying to beat him, but he knew he wasn't going to make it. He felt the blast alongside his head as Pino's rifle barked and sent the heavy lead ball, knocking the man backward off his feet, and it was over.

It had started and was over in no more than a few seconds, but Fran felt as if he had lived a lifetime in that short period.

Charley was standing in the doorway then, with his pistol when Fran approached. Looking at Fran, Charley said, "Everything is all right inside, Francis." Fran still wanted to see Angela, knowing that though she might not be hurt physically, she was surely distressed by what had just happened. He found her in the kitchen with Dove, who was saying that it was over, and that everything was all right.

They were holding each other, and he could see Angela was shaking as she turned and saw him standing with the blood on his shirt. Her demeanor changed completely, and she said, "You're wounded." Now both women came and made him sit up on the table. There they took off his shirt and checked the wound.

"It's just a scratch," he said, but Angela answered him, saying, "It's a bit more than that." Dove put his shirt in a bucket of cold water while Angela cleaned the wound; then they both worked on bandaging him, first around his middle and then over his shoulder to hold the dressing in place.

Pino came in and said he hung their rifles in the hall. Aleta and Cana were taking the packhorses to the cache, saying they, with the new family, would take care of the meat and hide. Charley had unsaddled the riding horses; then he said he'd go help Whistle dig the graves.

"Thanks for saving my neck out there, Pino," Fran said. "I might have taken another hit if I wasn't for you."

"I made two good shots today," Pino answered. "But so did you, Francis," he said as he left.

Fran sat at the table, his side hurting; it was all over, and he was beginning to feel tired and weak. Angela brought him a cup of coffee she'd laced with sugar and whiskey. It tasted good, and warmed him going down.

Charley came to tell him he'd taken care of the horses and the arms they carried. "I've put them on the counter, and I found their names going through their things," he said.

"Those men had been in the store before," Charley told them, "and must have seen where I had the cash box.

"You and Pino coming home broke up their little party. That fella knew I had a pistol under the counter too, and he told me to bring it out with my left hand.

"I think he would have put a bullet in me if Angela hadn't hollered; that's what gave me the chance to duck down. She saved my neck, Francis."

"And Pino saved mine," Fran said, "when, he took that same man out as he came out."

"Got to keep that quiet, Francis," Charley said. "Don't want anyone finding out an Indian took down a white man, even if it was to save someone else's skin.

"I'd better go see they get those crooks planted, but you stay put; this shouldn't take but a little while longer."

Fran felt tired but sat nursing a few more cups of just coffee while Angela and Dove worked in the kitchen.

He was almost asleep when everyone started coming in, the work that needed doing, done. The rest they could do tomorrow.

Angela brought Fran his supper and then sat down beside him. They sat on a bench, but she faced away from the table. Some of the fresh liver and wild onions fried on his plate, and he tried to give her a bite.

"I'm not really hungry," she said.

"Are you still nervous," Fran asked, "after screaming like that?"

"Yes, Francis," she answered. "You know, I could see you outside through the front window, and I thought I was going to see the father of my child shot down, right before my eyes."

Fran had just put a piece of liver into his mouth. He dropped his fork and, turning, put his arm out to draw her closer to him; she smiled and drew back, saying, "Please, Francis, finish chewing and swallow that before you kiss me."

The End

AUTHOR BIO

Born in San Francisco in 1925 a fourth generation Californian on his mother's side. Raised in Marin County he roamed the hills and the flats of the bay in sight of San Quentin. A veteran of World War Two serving in both, the Maritime Service, and the U S Army. Serving time overseas, aboard the M.V. Cape San Antonio. Later in the war serving in the Army the Hawaiian Division. The 24th Division, 34th Regiment, A company, 1st Platoon 1st Squad and for a time 1st Scout, in the Philippines

He raised four children working for Ma Bell 31 years and seven months in Marin and Santa Clara counties.

Hunted and fished from Lake Thomas Edison to the Oregon boarded in the Sierras, and from Los Padres National Forest to the Trinity Alps in the coast range, burro packing with his sons.

Spent seven years as a Boy Scout Leader and is an Honorary Life member of the PTA.

Has lived in Riverton Wyn, Sequim Wash. And rebuilt a cabin in Klawock Alaska on Prince of Wales island, where he hunted, fished and wrote in his spare moments.

He has 9 grand children, 10 great grand children plus a loved step daughter and daughter in law and two step grand children.